AN EXCERPT FROM
TRUST ME (ROUGH LOVE PART THREE)

It had been a month since I set out on my new career as a boutique jewelry designer. I'd amassed a backlog of beautiful gold and silver pieces, earrings, bracelets, necklaces...but no clients. Starshine, Ltd. had received exactly one order since its inception, and that order came from Price—two bracelets with attachment points for chains, in the style of manacles. On the order form he wrote *Must stand up to the frenzied pulling of a one hundred and twenty pound woman in the course of a long and grueling punishment session.*

I weighed a hundred and twenty pounds. I'd failed to find my first customer by the end of August.

Yes. I was fabricating a pair of shackles for myself.

I deserved to be punished, because after three years at one of New York's top art schools, I'd fallen way short in launching my career. I'd lamed out, full stop. I'd been more concerned with being my Master's slave and obsessing over his poetry than bringing my jewelry designs to the world. The whole reason he'd held me at arm's length for three years was so this wouldn't happen.

I frowned and fitted one of the manacles around my wrist. I didn't want them to be stark metal bonds, but works of art. I wanted these instruments of torture to be pretty and exquisitely fitted. I wanted something good to come out of this. I wanted to please the man I thought of as both my Master and soul mate, but the project was also shadowed by sadness. I wasn't measuring up to our unspoken agreement, and he was calling me on it. I was scared about what that meant.

I clicked the clasp together and wiggled the manacle on my wrist. The fit was true. The design was pretty.

So why wasn't I happy?

"A Chorus Girl" by E.E. Cummings was originally published in *Eight Harvard Poets*, New York, Laurence J. Gomme, 1917. It is used in this work by rights of public domain:

TRUST
ME

ROUGH LOVE PART THREE

ANNABEL JOSEPH

Other Books by Annabel Joseph

Mercy
Cait and the Devil
Firebird
Owning Wednesday
Lily Mine
Disciplining the Duchess

Fortune series:
Deep in the Woods
Fortune

Comfort series:
Comfort Object
Caressa's Knees
Odalisque
Command Performance

Cirque Masters series:
Cirque de Minuit
Bound in Blue
Master's Flame

Mephisto series:
Club Mephisto
Molly's Lips: Club Mephisto Retold
Burn For You

BDSM Ballet series:
Waking Kiss
Fever Dream

Properly Spanked series:
Training Lady Townsend
To Tame A Countess
My Naughty Minette
Under A Duke's Hand

CHAPTER ONE:
OWNED

Once upon a time, there was a lost, lonely princess, and a rough-edged prince who owned a castle with a dungeon. The dungeon was hidden away behind a secret door, but the princess knew it was there because it had become the center of their relationship. It was okay.

Mostly okay.

In fact, the princess dreamed about the dungeon as much as she dreamed about the prince. She loved and hated both of them, her dreams a peculiar mixture of happiness and dread. Sometimes the prince tormented her, whipped her or choked her while he whispered lurid threats in her ear, but sometimes he gave her poetry, real poetry he'd written only for her.

You lean over your work
Lips pursed, then moving
Whispering unintelligible words of affection
As you bring beauty to the world

I ran my fingers over the paper that lay front and center on my worktable, reading his words when I should have been working. I was the princess, even though most days I didn't feel like it. I still persisted. I wanted happily ever after with my prince.

That was complicated too.

I folded the poem and put it in a drawer with the others, and refocused on my work, on the two gleaming silver ovals in front of me. My studio was quiet today. Sometimes I listened to an eclectic playlist as I worked with my metals and soldering irons, but today I worked in silence because I was a failure, undeserving of music.

As promised, Price had given me some money to start my jewelry business, and rented a space for me a couple floors below his office. My studio had only two rooms: a front room where I worked and stored my supplies, and a back room done up as a lounge for prospective clients, with large, comfortable chairs and a central table for setting out samples and discussing designs. So far, the only person I'd met with in there was Price. Most of the time the back room sat empty, the light from the single window moving across the carpet and chairs.

It had been a month since I set out on my new career as a boutique jewelry designer. I'd amassed a backlog of beautiful gold and silver pieces, earrings, bracelets, necklaces...but no clients. Starshine, Ltd. had received exactly one order since its inception, and that order came from Price— two bracelets with attachment points for chains, in the style of manacles. On the order form he wrote *Must stand up to the frenzied pulling of a one hundred and twenty pound woman in the course of a long and grueling punishment session.*

I weighed a hundred and twenty pounds. I'd failed to find my first customer by the end of August.

Yes. I was fabricating a pair of shackles for myself.

I deserved to be punished, because after three years at one of New York's top art schools, I'd fallen way short in launching my career. I'd lamed out, full stop. I'd been more concerned with being my Master's slave and obsessing over his poetry than bringing my jewelry designs to the world. The whole reason he'd held me at arm's length for three years was so this wouldn't happen.

I frowned and fitted one of the manacles around my wrist. I didn't want them to be stark metal bonds, but works of art. I wanted these instruments of torture to be pretty and exquisitely fitted. I wanted something good to come out of this. I wanted to please the man I thought of as both my Master and soul mate, but the project was also shadowed by sadness. I wasn't measuring up to our unspoken agreement, and he was calling me on it. I was scared about what that meant.

I clicked the clasp together and wiggled the manacle on my wrist. The fit was true. The design was pretty.

So why wasn't I happy?

I took it off and arranged it on the table beside the other manacle with a carefully calculated distance between them, connected by a chain. It was a metaphor for us, because we were connected, but not really together. He said he loved me, but he didn't love me yet. He didn't trust me, or perhaps he didn't trust himself, and earning that trust was going to be a long and complicated process on top of everything else. Clients were the last thing on my mind. My career didn't seem that important anymore, when our relationship was in this shifting stage of vulnerability.

The door swung open. Only one person came here, and he never knocked. In the big, wide world he was P.T. Eriksen, famous architect, but when I wasn't calling him Sir, I called him Price. He was tall and strong, with piercing blue eyes and blond hair, and bold, expressive features. At the moment, those features were deliciously intent. He locked the door behind him, then strode toward the back room, not even glancing at the manacles. He was already shrugging off his suit jacket. I jumped to my feet and followed.

As soon as I entered the back room, he was on me, grasping me, holding my head in hard fingers, as if he had to force me to endure his kisses. I moaned because I wanted those kisses. He came to visit me at least once a day, sometimes more, for this, for kisses and groping and fast, hard sex against the wall or over the couch, or sprawled out on the carpet.

His force ruled my world. All he had to do was touch me—grab me—and I melted for him. I ground my hips against his crotch as he yanked up my skirt. I was only allowed to wear skirts or dresses to work now, with no panties underneath. It was a very effective method of making me think about him all day. At home, I wasn't allowed to wear anything at all, except nipple clamps, harnesses, chastity devices, and other evil things he used to torment me. In comparison, the no-panty rule was positively tame, and it allowed him easy access during these fleeting visits.

He forced me to my knees and I undid his fly, releasing his thick erection. He thrust into my mouth with his pants still around his hips. I held up his shirt, being very careful to keep him neat and clean, because once he left me, he'd go back to work in his office upstairs. My old friends at Eriksen Architectural Design knew I had a studio here, and that their boss came to visit me. They knew we were together, since he'd taken me to a couple of corporate dinners. Why wouldn't the boss fall for the intern? They didn't know the rest of our three-year history. Maybe that was for the best.

I choked, a loss of concentration. He twisted fingers in my hair and pulled hard to refocus me. *Yes, yes, Sir, forgive me.* I didn't say it out loud, didn't say anything, just went back to sucking him. We hadn't shared so much as a greeting yet, but that wasn't unusual when his mind was on sex. He didn't like a bunch of words clouding up the dynamic between us. When we were in his dungeon, I wasn't allowed to speak at all. Not one word, not one syllable unless I was responding to a question. He'd told me that rule the first day, and no amount of protesting and negotiation had changed his mind. After being gagged many times over the following week, sometimes for more than an hour, I'd learned to accept it and obey.

But I could still make noises. I could scream and whine, yelp and shriek, groan and struggle to my heart's content. And here, now, I could talk, because this wasn't the dungeon, but what was there to say except *Use me*, and *I missed you*, and *I love you, even when you treat me this way…*

His hands tightened in my hair until my toes curled in my shoes, then he released me and nudged me toward the sofa. I crawled there, waiting for his hands to show me what he wanted. He lifted me and bent me over the cushions, slapped my ass and shoved his cock inside me. I was so, so wet. His forceful thrusts banged my hips against the couch where I should have been meeting with clients. Let's face it, I was way better at having sex than launching a business.

"Hurt me," I whispered into my hands. "Please hurt me."

I wanted to touch myself, but I didn't. He could make me come from fucking alone, from rubbing over my G-spot until my legs were trembling and my clit was swollen into a throbbing, horny center of need. I didn't have to ask permission to come, but I was sometimes instructed not to come, intentionally or on a whim. This created a situation where I tried to come all the time, until he told me not to—because at any moment he might tell me not to.

He enjoyed my scrabbling, frenzied attempts to get off, enjoyed making me come over and over sometimes, until I was exhausted. I bucked back against him, ignoring the scratching carpet against my knees, but constantly aware of keeping his clothes clean. The one time I'd accidentally humped his pants and left a wet spot, he'd made me take them to the dry cleaner with a very sore ass. Live and learn. Since I'd moved in with Price, I'd learned so many things.

Be good. Be a pleasing, sexually available slave. Hurt for Master when he wants it. Don't ask him if he loves you.

"Oh, please," I said. "I'm so close."

He immediately changed his rhythm to make it harder for me to come. I should have known better by now than to admit I was almost there. He squeezed my nipples through my shirt, making my pussy twitch and clench around his cock. He was so big, he filled me so full. He was everything to me. He left my nipples and reached down to slap my clit. The contact felt electric. I stuffed my knuckles in my mouth so I wouldn't ask for it again, because then I might not get it. He slapped my clit again, hurting me as much as he thrilled me. The third time I went off, climaxing, grinding on his hand as he drilled into me.

See, some women were into soft caresses and gently whispered endearments. Not me. And it wasn't because I'd worked as a stripper and a call girl, or that I didn't realize my value, or that I came from an abusive home and was somehow messed up in the head. It was because I was wired to enjoy violence, and Price was wired to enjoy giving it to me. His thrusts intensified, marking me, invading me, and then I heard him come too with the rough growls that signaled his climax.

I hated when it was over, because that meant he would let go and leave my body. The waiting would begin, the craving for his next possession. How was I supposed to go out there and keep working?

He squeezed my shoulder and I turned to do my task, cleaning him up with my lips and tongue so he could shove his cock back into his pants and return to work too.

"Go fix yourself up," he said when I finished. "Then I need to see you out in the other room."

I went into the powder room and did what I could about the jizz and juices dripping out of me. It was impossible to be someone's sex slave and retain the full measure of your pride. There were a lot of indignities, bodily fluids and hurried cleanup sessions, and pulling your skirt down over your bare ass and pussy and getting on with your day. When I went into the other room, Price stood by my worktable looking down at the manacles.

"You promised delivery today," he said. "Are they finished?"

"Yes, Sir." I hurried over to show him, but he stopped me.

"Not yet," he murmured. "Sit."

I sat in my desk chair and he pulled a second chair up right beside me. I wanted him to look over at the manacles and like them, maybe even compliment them, but he looked at me instead. I swallowed and clasped my hands in my lap, one hundred percent aware that this sinfully handsome man had been ramming his cock into my body not five minutes earlier. It might as well have been five hours ago. No more fun time.

This was going to be rough.

"We need to talk about your lack of progress," he said.

Do we have to? my brain whined. My lips remained shut.

"What have you been doing?" he prompted, looking around my organized workspace.

"I've been making things."

My studio smelled similar to the old metals lab at Norton, although I think this building had better ventilation. I slid a glance at the manacles, and showed him some earrings I'd been working on before then, with tiny, deep blue, speckled stones. He didn't look that impressed.

"They're pretty," he said. "Who's going to wear them?"

"I don't know. I just like making stuff. I don't feel comfortable pushing it on people."

"Artists want their art to be seen. You're making excuses. You're being lazy."

I grimaced. "Thanks."

"I've introduced you to dozens of people in the last few weeks. You've had plenty of chances to sell yourself."

It was the wrong choice of words, considering I'd literally sold myself for ten years, whored myself out to hundreds of clients. I blinked and stared down at my interlaced fingers.

"I gave you extra time," he said. "I gave you until the end of August. You knew what I expected. One customer. One person interested enough in your brand and your talent to commission a piece. One fucking bracelet, Chere. A pair of gold studs. One fucking ring."

Every word he said made me feel smaller. Ugh, why couldn't talent and creativity be enough? Why did I have to sell myself? "I'd rather work for someone else," I said. "I appreciate you setting me up here and everything, but I don't want the responsibility of running my own company. I decided I don't really like that. I mean, it was your idea."

I chanced a glance at him. He regarded me with unsettling focus.

"I'm not a marketer," I protested as the stare wore me down. "I'm not a salesperson."

"Then learn how to be a salesperson, or hire some salespeople to work for you."

"I don't know how. We didn't learn those skills at art school."

"You saw me work with people during your internship," he reminded me. "You sat in on countless meetings and watched me do dozens of deals. You watched me network and put projects together."

"Yes, and you're great at it. You're great at getting shit done and convincing people they need your buildings and bridges. I'm making classic, elegant pieces of jewelry that no one's interested in. I've got no hook. I've got no flair. I'm not a business person." His eyes darkened with each denial. I could barely hold his gaze. "You can't punish me for sucking at business."

"I can punish you for being so fucking negative. I can punish you for anything I like."

His big, capable hands rested in his lap. He was going to hurt me later with those hands because I was lame and uncertain, and not making any progress. I was failing to launch.

"I feel horrible. I hate disappointing you," I said, trying to elicit some sympathy. "It's hard to have you connected to my working world, my art."

"I'm connected to whatever I want, as far as you're concerned. That was the deal we made, remember? You belong to me, body and soul."

I looked around my workroom, at everything he'd made possible. I loved belonging to him, but at the same time, I was a failure, a disappointment, an underperformer who had to be punished. My friend Andrew had graduated at the same time as me, and he was already selling lots of his work.

"Sometimes I think I don't want to do the jewelry anymore," I said, looking back at him. "I just want to belong to you."

I knew that would make him furious. It was exactly what he hadn't wanted to happen. It was the whole reason he'd resisted letting me into his life, but now I was in his life and all I wanted to do was serve him. He'd paid a lot of money to help me become a designer, and now I didn't want to design. He could force me to do it. He could force me to do anything in our dynamic, and I had no safe words to extricate myself.

He let out a long, sad breath, then reached to pick up one of the manacles I'd made. He turned it over in his hand and reached for my wrist. It worked on a delicate, hidden hinge, closing snugly around my skin and bones. I'd fashioned it with curved edges, but I hadn't added any kind of padding. I didn't deserve padding.

"You know I love you, Chere," he said, fingering the clasp. To my ears, it sounded like he was trying to convince himself. I didn't believe him. I didn't trust him, which made me a very bad slave.

He closed the manacle with a snap and studied it on my wrist. I'd polished it until it shone. Without the fitting for the chain, the silver band could pass for a bracelet. He picked up the other one and put it on me so my wrists were tethered by the chain. He brought them together and covered my hands with his, and held them as he gazed into my eyes.

"These are beautiful," he said, and it sounded like the sad breath he'd taken earlier. "You do beautiful work. The world needs this work."

I tried to read his expression. I saw disappointment and doubt. Was he questioning us? Questioning whether he needed to let me go? The words burst out of me in a panic.

"Don't leave me. Don't make me go away."

He released my hands and grabbed my face. I flinched as his fingertips dug into my cheeks. "Do you think I'd do that to you?"

"You *did* do it to me. You left me before. Twice."

He gave me a harsh look, followed by a brisk slap on the cheek. It was hard to hold his gaze, but when my eyes slid away he grabbed my neck and I knew I'd better fucking attend to him. I didn't know what I feared more, his punishment or his desertion. If he believed he was harming me, he would leave me. I knew that. He'd done it before.

Twice.

"I'm sorry," I pleaded. "I'll do better. I just want to be with you. The jewelry design, the business, it takes away from my time with you."

"You used to love making jewelry."

"Now I love you."

I felt his fingers tighten. "We have plenty of time together outside of work. You need a life besides being my—"

He stopped talking, but I knew him well enough to understand the things he didn't say. He wanted me to maintain a life outside of our claustrophobic emotional entanglement in case we had to part again. I knew he maintained escape plans. My career was one of them, because it prevented my complete surrender. My eyes filled with tears.

"Don't leave me," I whispered, turning my neck to get more air. "Please."

A muscle in his jaw ticked. "Don't tell me what to do."

We sat like that for fifteen seconds or more, staring at one another with his hand around my neck. I clasped my fingers together and the manacles clinked.

"I'll find a client by next week," I promised. "I'll do whatever it takes."

"We're leaving for Paris in two days."

"When we get back, then. I'll use that time in Paris to create a marketing plan—"

"You don't even know what a marketing plan is." He let go of my neck and looked at my work. "You need to be out in the world, getting inspired, talking to people, telling them about your vision."

But I want to be in your dungeon. I want to be near you, loving you. I want you to love me...

"I'll visit jewelry shops in Paris," I promised. "I'll go to fashion shows. I'll keep working if you want me to work."

"I want you to work." He looked back at me, pinning me with his stern, blue gaze. "You can do both, be my slave and share your talents with the world. Your job," he said, pointing his finger at me, "is to do what I think is best for you. I don't want you to lose yourself inside me, inside my house and my life and my will. Inside my dungeon."

"Yes, Sir," I said dutifully, but the tears were back, because he'd just described exactly what I wanted. It was what he wanted too. He'd told me as much when he came back into my life, but he wouldn't allow himself such selfish pleasure.

"What?" he snapped. "Why are you crying?"

"Because you're angry with me. And because..."

His finger tapped on his knee. I wasn't looking forward to the punishment later, but if I was getting it anyway, I might as well speak my mind.

"I'm crying because I think you don't... I think you don't really want me. You don't want our relationship."

I put my hands up to cover my eyes. He yanked them back down with the chain. "Why the fuck would you say that?"

"You want me to work so I'll be able to support myself when you leave. You're not going to stay with me."

He pursed his lips, his eyes flashing fire. His grip tightened on the chain. "You're mine, Chere, and I intend to keep you. But our deal was for you to maintain a creative life too, a real life with a real job."

"I don't want a real job. I want to belong to you—"

"You do belong to me," he interrupted, not even allowing me to finish my plea. "Now shut the fuck up. I'm tired of your whining." He turned over my wrists and worked the clasp to open the manacles. "You can leave at three o'clock to go home and prepare yourself. I'll be home around six."

"Yes, Sir."

He slipped the manacles into his pocket and tipped up my chin. "This isn't going to be a fun night for you, starshine. When I threatened punishment, I meant punishment. I'm not happy with you." He brushed away one of my tears. "But that doesn't mean I don't want you, or that I wish you would leave. Don't put words in my mouth or tell me what I'm going to do as far as you're concerned, because I do what I want, and you fucking accept it. It's very simple," he said, pointing at his chest. "I own you. Your only job is to fucking be owned."

CHAPTER TWO:
PUNISHMENT

I left at three, as instructed. That was really when the punishment started, because my thoughts, from that point on, were fixated on the pain I had coming to me, and the fear of what he might make me endure.

I undressed and put my clothes in the guest room, as I did every day. The guest room was the vanilla room where things like clothes and belongings were kept, because in his bedroom and his dungeon I was purely his naked, obedient slave. He said the separation was necessary, that I couldn't be doing things like getting dressed and checking my email in his bedroom. It would make us too equal, too much like some boring, traditional couple.

God forbid we would be that.

Once I was naked, I ate a snack and drank some water. I had a long soak in the tub, preparing all the various parts of my body for use and abuse. I used to do a similar routine before I went on dates with him, when I was a high priced escort. Back then, it had been work, routine. Now it was the manic desire to please him, even when I'd displeased him.

After the bath, I got my collar from his bedside table and buckled it around my neck. It was comforting to put on the circle of soft, brown leather. It was also a reminder that I needed to trust him and stop worrying about how he was feeling and whether he would leave me. If I belonged to him, truly belonged to him, none of that mattered. His will was my will, end of story. I felt embarrassed now for my neurotic display, my tears and whining.

I definitely deserved to be punished.

It wouldn't be the first time I'd earned a punishment. He'd turned out to be a very exacting Master, with no qualms about making me cry when I broke his rules. He supplied good rough and bad rough. The quick, sexy fuck in the back room of my studio had been good rough. Punishments were bad rough, pushing me beyond boundaries, and tapping reserves of strength I didn't know I had.

I lotioned myself up really well, including my nipples, which were sure to receive plenty of abuse. After that, there was nothing left to do but wait and stress, and mull over my life choices. I drifted into the guest room and lifted a stack of pillows in the closet, and took out the pair of binoculars secreted there.

He'd never specifically told me that I couldn't use the binoculars, but I was furtive when I borrowed them, and I always put them back under the pillows as if they'd never been disturbed. I took them out to the living room and focused on my old apartment across the street. Someone else was living there now, a boring, traditional couple that I spied on from time to time. They might be boring, but they were also happy. I was supposed to be happy too.

Oh, hell. I was happy. I was just scared of losing him again, because it had happened too many times before. I kept his poetry in a special scrapbook, in the same closet where he kept the binoculars, and I clung to those heartfelt poems as evidence that everything was okay. He wrote the poems himself now. They were short and sweet, and wonderful.

I lowered the binoculars. The couple wasn't there right now. I rested my head against the glass and wondered if anyone was spying on me, the worried looking girl whose brown hair and brown eyes matched her brown slave collar. I had to stop worrying. I had to stop expecting him to desert me. I'd asked him to trust me, and the flip side of that was that I had to trust him.

I went back to the guest room and hid the binoculars, took one last look at my appearance, and went into his room. He had a chair in there, a hard wooden chair where I was expected to wait for him at least ten minutes prior to his expected arrival. *Back straight, feet on the floor, hands in your lap. You'll be there ten minutes before you expect me, not eight minutes, or five minutes.*

The first few days I lived here, he'd taught me a hundred rules, a hundred expectations for my behavior when I was in our slave space—his bedroom and the dungeon beyond. There were rules about my hair (always down, never up), about my jewelry (nothing but stud earrings), about when I could look away from him (never, in the dungeon), about when I could talk (never, in the dungeon). Respectful talk in the bedroom was allowed, but it was at my own risk. If I annoyed him, I paid the price.

The respect spilled out of the bedroom into other areas of our life. Sometimes, at company dinners or events, I almost called him Sir. That was a no-no. I was careful what I said to him, unlike the times before, when I spoke more freely. The times before, meaning before slavery and ownership and the consuming control he exercised over me now. I'd wanted that control. I'd begged for it. I checked the collar to be sure the O-ring was at the front, and listened for the sound of him at the door.

He arrived within a few minutes of six o'clock and found me sitting as I was supposed to be, back straight, feet on the floor, hands in my lap. He strolled over to me as I drank him up with my eyes. *Master, please master me. Please punish me so we can start fresh again and I can do things right.*

When he reached me, he clasped my neck and tilted my face up for a kiss. That kiss was for being where I was supposed to be, doing what I was supposed to be doing. It didn't last.

He pulled away and turned his back on me, shrugged off his suit jacket and disappeared into the closet. He reappeared in a pair of jeans and nothing else, such a flawless specimen of enticing masculinity that I could have sobbed. His abs were flat and hard, and his jeans rode just below his hips to showcase perfect iliac furrows. I flushed as he crossed to me, all business.

"Are you ready?" he asked.

"Yes, Sir."

"You understand why you're being punished?"

"Yes, Sir. I'm being punished for not being more proactive in my business. For not...for not working harder at getting my art out into the world."

He studied me a moment, with an intensity that made me squirm. "All it takes is inspiration. You of all people should know that." He touched my cheek, a soft touch before the storm. "Maybe I can inspire you. Or at least light a fire under your ass. Hold out your arms."

He pulled the manacles I'd made from his pocket. I let out a slow breath as he secured them around my wrists, closing each clasp with a click. I was sure he'd used the words "fire" and "ass" with intentional purpose. My ass, as they say, was grass, as was any other part of my body he thought suitable for punishment tonight.

"All right," he said, taking my arm. "Come on."

He led me through his closet to the dungeon room, an echoing, concrete-walled chamber of racks, benches, and polished furniture. Once inside, he nudged me toward the tall chests where he kept all his hurtiest equipment. I had to wait there while he moved about the dungeon turning on lamps and recessed spotlights to illuminate my shame.

When the frightening disciplinary space was awash in light, he returned and opened a drawer to take out a ball gag. He turned to me. No words necessary. I took my last few breaths of unimpeded air and opened my mouth. The ball was hard and black, and large enough to depress my tongue. He buckled it behind my head and turned back to the drawers. He pulled out a butt plug next, a glass one with a painfully wide base. I gave a little moan that wasn't audible through the gag, not that any moan or groan would make him soften his plans.

"Go bend over the bench," he ordered.

I obeyed, crawling onto the lower step and then folding myself over the raised center platform. My ass felt very vulnerable, as he meant it to. I knew that butt plug would hurt. Too soon, he was behind me, forcing me to spread my legs wider with a series of punishing slaps to my inner thighs. Once I was positioned to his liking, he parted my cheeks and shoved cold, slippery lube into my asshole. He wasn't gentle, but I was grateful that he was being generous with the lube, considering the size of the plug.

After he finished preparing my ass, he spread my cheeks wide and held them open. I closed my eyes as I felt the hard tip of the toy against my hole. He worked it in and out, causing a little more pain each time. Even though he trained my ass with plugs and dildos, and even though he frequently fucked me there, it was still a struggle every time. I whined and pushed out as he nudged the widest part of the base against my ass. He had to stop and add more lube. I wanted to move, to squirm away, but I didn't dare.

Surrender. It's supposed to feel bad. This is a punishment.

I cried behind the gag as he started moving the plug in and out again, all the way to the widest part. The long, rough fingers of his other hand pressed into my skin as he held my cheeks open. Finally, with an aching stab of pain, he shoved the anal toy home. I clenched around the base, relieved that the acute pain was over, but there was still the discomfort of having a large, heavy bulb seated in my ass, and surely more anal torment to come.

He walked around the bench and I raised my eyes to look at him. If he wasn't behind me, or on top of me, I was supposed to meet his gaze. I tried to swallow. The first bits of drool gathered at the corners of my lips but I wasn't allowed to wipe it away.

"Does that hurt, bad girl?" he asked.

God, yes, it hurt to be bad. I nodded, trying to communicate how sad and sorry I was. He stood over me, my figure of authority, my owner.

"Fifty with the paddle to begin."

My whole body cringed. He put a finger in my collar's O-ring and dragged my torso down to rest right on the upper platform. He unhooked the manacles from their connecting chain and fixed one wrist to either side of the spanking bench so my arms were spread wide. Spread wide in every way, I thought ruefully, as I clenched on the plug inside me.

"Keep your fucking ass in the air," he said, walking to stand behind me. He gave me some warm up spanks, pausing now and again to force me to arch my back. "And keep those legs spread, so I can paddle your thighs too."

I dropped my head, wishing this was over rather than just beginning. The warm up spanks stopped, and I sensed rather than heard him pick up the paddle. This wasn't playtime. It was punishment, and he went to town. He spanked one cheek at a time, avoiding the plug's base. It wasn't a big paddle, but the small, thick ones could be brutal. Each blow was hot, stinging fire, and I squealed behind the gag. I was supposed to stay still and I did my best, but I couldn't control the trembling in my legs or the frantic movement of my feet.

"Ass out," he scolded whenever I tried to cower in a self-protective way.

I lost count of the paddle strokes after the first dozen or so. I couldn't keep up; I was just trying to hold it together. When my cheeks burned beyond bearing, he moved to the backs of my upper thighs, and it absolutely killed like hellfire. *Ow, ow, ow, ow...* I yanked at the manacles I'd so carefully crafted, and wiggled my ass back and forth to try to lessen the ratcheting pain.

"Be still," he warned, spanking me harder as punishment.

I braced myself against the bench and cried behind the gag, knowing there would be no lessening, no stopping until he was done. At last, the sharp cracks of the paddle died out in the quiet dungeon. I went limp against the platform, and watched a stream of drool drip from the gag down to the floor beneath me.

"I know it hurts," he said, squeezing my ass cheeks. "That's the only way you'll learn. That's the only way you'll do better."

I moaned in agreement, wondering what would be next. It turned out to be a strap, a narrow, supple piece of leather he used on me a lot. Again, he punished my hurting bottom and then the sensitive skin at the apex of my thighs. I imagine he gave me fifty more. It felt like a thousand and I started bawling.

"Spread your legs wider," he said, unmoved. "As wide as they'll go."

When I complied, he used the strap on my inner thighs. I screeched behind the gag, grateful now that he'd put it on me, because I didn't think I would have been able to hold back the words screaming in my head. *Stop, stop. Oh my fucking God in heaven, stop torturing me.*

By the time he put the strap away, my entire backside and upper legs were on fire. The butt plug was an afterthought. It still didn't feel good, but it felt better than having my ass paddled and my inner thighs strapped until they burned. I prayed the punishment was over, but I was pretty sure I wouldn't be that lucky.

I watched him as he came around to release my wrists, but he didn't meet my gaze. Instead he chained my manacles back together and twisted the metal links in his fist. I was forced up off the bench and walked over to the ladder rack affixed to the wall. I felt the heavy plug in my ass with each step. He made me stand with my back against the rack while he attached my wrists high over my head. My breasts were forced forward and I had to stand on the balls of my feet.

I watched him cross to the chests of implements and return with a crop and a clear Lucite cane. *Oh shit, oh shit.* While my throbbing ass bumped against the rack's bars, he flicked my breasts with the crop. I threw my head back for a moment, breaking eye contact, but there was no way to escape. The tip of the crop connected with my nipples over and over, sharp bites of pain on my most sensitive, delicate skin. *At least he's not using clamps*, I thought miserably, but then I thought, *those will be next, when my nipples are already hurt.*

I returned my gaze to his face because I was supposed to keep my attention on him in the dungeon, whether he was giving me agony or bliss. This was agony. His eyes were hard and intent. He didn't miss a nipple once. When they felt painful enough to fall off, he put down the crop and picked up the cane. I glanced warily at the thin, whippy tool, then returned my eyes to his face.

I got five cane strokes against the fronts of my thighs, while I screamed and jerked and danced on my faltering toes. Every time he hit me, it felt like he was slicing me open. By the end of the cane strokes I was so frantic and clenched up that the plug felt huge in my ass again.

I caught his gaze and pleaded with my eyes. *Please, please, I'm sorry I failed you. I'll do better. This hurts so much.* Tears streamed down my face. He stared at me, stern as ever. "I could be harder on you, you know," he said. "I could tear you up, but I won't, because I love you."

That made me cry harder. He ran fingers through my tears, smearing them in with my drool. "Cry all you want," he said gently. "I won't let you get away."

* * * * *

She was fucking poetry.

Chere was poetry in my dungeon, fixed to my bondage rack. I sighed, then leaned down and kissed her cheek, tasting her tears.

"We're not done yet," I said, massaging her reddened nipples. "I'm going to fuck your ass now. Hard. I'm going to punish you with my cock."

She gave me a sad, pleading look, but she knew I'd stick to my plan. I released her arms and took her over to the toy chests. I opened the drawer with all the nipple clamps and let her take a good look. Today, she was getting awful ones. I toyed with her nipples, enjoying her gasping and flinching. I took out a pair of heavy black clover clamps that would tug like hell when I bent her over and subjected her to a rough assfucking.

Bad slaves got punished. I'd warned her that the deadline was approaching, and she'd decided not to act. I was the kind of Master who punished every infraction, no matter how small, and her failure wasn't a small thing.

"Stand up straight," I said. "I'm not going to fight with you over these clamps. Keep your hands down and stick your tits out."

She did, but she was still crying, still scared. Her chest quailed with her sobs, but that was the point of punishment, to use pain to teach her a lesson. I clamped the first nipple as she squealed behind the gag. The walls were soundproof, thank God. Gag or not, she was making a racket. I clamped the other nipple and let the chain fall down between her breasts. She stared at me as I did it. She was required to look at me, as a power thing, yes, but a safety thing too. I decided she was eighty percent done, but she had a little more hurt and humiliation to endure. I marched her over to the sawhorse and bent her over it, hooking the chain of her manacles to an attachment point on the floor.

She squealed again as the position caused the heavy, hanging clamps to yank down on her nipples. Poor baby. Well, she was the one who'd fallen in love with a sadist. That kind of love came with a price.

"Stop that whining," I said, yanking her head back by the hair. This, too, jostled the clamps and increased her pain. I kicked her legs apart, spread her wide open, and shackled her ankles to the bottom of the horse. The plug came out next. Big, glass plugs couldn't be comfortable for her, but at least they stretched her open a little before I commenced the anal portion of her ordeal. I stripped and lubed myself up, and took her hips in my hands, and pushed against her clenching hole.

Her little muscle resisted, but not much. Her ass was still scarlet from the paddling, and I made sure to squeeze her cheeks painfully as I drove into her, inch by inch.

Maybe you think I'm too cruel. Maybe you think I'm a bastard. Yeah, I'm both of those things, but she was here, and she accepted the sadistic side of me like the hardcore masochist she was.

Once I was seated all the way in her ass, I added more lube and settled in for a rough, prolonged fuck. Ten minutes. I never left those kinds of clamps on her for more than ten minutes, and a couple of minutes had already gone by, but eight minutes of rough assfucking probably felt like an hour to her, so it would be enough.

Oh, God, she felt so good on my cock. Her sphincter clenched around me, sending shock waves to my balls. She was bound and impaled, my hurting creature. Now and again she'd squirm over the padded top of the horse, which was naughty, but hell, it increased my pleasure. Let her squirm. She wasn't getting off this ride until I let her go.

Pretty soon, I started to feel like I was going to come, and it was too soon, so I pulled out of her and went for the strap. I gave her a few swats across the ass, and was rewarded with lovely moaning. I changed the angle and landed a couple strokes on her glistening, exposed pussy. She bucked her hips and jerked her legs in their bonds.

So beautiful. I plunged back into her ass, hurting her, taking her. After a minute or two of hard fucking, I pulled out again and strapped her, just on her pussy this time. *Agh, agh, agh*, such beautiful protesting sounds, and of course, every time I made her jerk, it hurt her nipples worse.

Chere, the things you endure for me. I love you so much.

I pushed back into her ass, reveling in her body's trembling acquiescence. I slowed down, enjoying the final deep strokes before my climax exploded. I covered her with my body, sliding over her warm, damp skin. Her punished cheeks felt hot against my hips as I embraced her. I emptied myself inside her, feeling a little sad about how much I hurt her, but feeling glowing contentment too.

Punishment, Price. This is a punishment, not cuddle time.

I pulled away from her and took a moment to remove the nipple clamps before I went to wash up. She waited there, bound and crying. Poor little slave. She should have tried harder to sell herself as a designer. I meant for her to find success, because I was determined that our dynamic not rob her of her greater purpose in life. She was going to make it, if I had to do rough anal to her every fucking week to motivate her.

25

Ah. Rough anal every week.

I shook off the fantasies and returned to my bound penitent. I decided she should spend a little time straddling the bad-girl sawhorse to really drive my point home. I put a new, even larger plug in her ass and unbound her so I could turn the top of the horse to the peaked side. The rounded edge would dig mercilessly into her girly parts and make her very sorry for her crimes.

I positioned her on the horse and bound her hands up over her head so she couldn't slouch or squirm away from the discomfort. Her feet didn't quite touch the ground. There was no more pleading in her gaze when she looked at me, only exhausted submission. Her face was a mess of tears, and her chest was a mess of drool. I took off the gag and cleaned her up as she struggled on top of the sawhorse.

"Don't be a baby," I said, ignoring her mewling cries. "You earned this. Ten minutes."

That caused more crying. I grabbed her collar and kissed her, taking her sobs into my mouth. "Everything hurts, doesn't it?" I asked as I pulled away. "Your ass hurts, your nipples hurt. Your thighs hurt." I traced one of the five pink welts on her straining legs. "And it hurts inside you, doesn't it? That big plug, just after I reamed you with my cock? And of course, your pussy hurts."

I slid my fingers between her pussy and the structure digging into her labia. I found her wet, engorged clit. "It hurts, doesn't it, baby? You can answer me."

"Yes, Sir."

Her voice sounded weak. She was ninety-eight percent done now. Maybe ninety-nine percent. Edging her would be too much. I stopped stroking her clit and shoved my finger in her mouth. She sucked it clean so prettily that I kissed her again. There's something about kissing your slave when she's crying and going out of her mind...

The last five minutes, I just stood back and watched her, this gorgeous, masochistic woman who'd transformed my life. I admired her chestnut curls, gazed into her striking brown eyes, and adored every pale freckle on her face. Why didn't she understand how much I loved her, how much it would take to make me leave her? Her self-destruction, nothing less. I had to keep that from happening, even if it took extreme punishment sessions like this.

When the ten minutes were up, I helped her off the horse, took off her pretty manacles, and led her back into my bedroom. I turned on the shower and pulled her under the water to clean her up. She was trembly and melting, clinging to my shoulders. *I love you*, she whispered over and over. *I'm sorry.* I hushed her and licked a trail up her neck, and kissed her hotly and deeply with water running down between our lips.

When we got out of the shower, I dried her off and studied the damage I'd wrought. Nothing permanent, but she had some garish marks. I stroked her pussy and asked if it was sore from the horse, only because I wanted to listen to her soft, sad voice say "Yes, Sir." We went back into the dungeon to straighten up the toys and put them away in their respective drawers, and the hurting part was over.

You survived. Good girl.

I threw on some jeans and a tee shirt and led Chere out to the living room. I had her sit at my feet while I ordered takeout from a local Italian place. She rested her head against my leg, exhausted. I played with her curls and read a book until the food arrived.

It was a good night for a quiet dinner in. Chere cried through most of it, unable to sit still in her chair. I drew her into my lap instead, and fed her Chicken Parmesan from my plate while she sniffled and trembled.

"That's enough now," I said. "Eat a little more." And she did, because I was her Master, and I had power over her for as long as we played this game.

After dinner was cleared away, I sent her to her bedroom and went back into the dungeon, over to my evil chests of torture instruments. I opened the drawer with the harnesses and chastity belts, and took out the one without the butt plug attachment. She'd probably endured enough anal punishment for one night.

When I brought the chastity belt into her room, Chere paled, but made no protest. She whined a lot less these days. She was a lot less self-protective. She used to cower when I presented shit like this, and cross her arms in front of her. Now, even after all I'd put her through, her arms rarely left her side.

I studied her, fingering the metal plate that would lock away her clit and pussy and prevent any stolen pleasures. "You probably don't need this tonight," I said.

She shuddered. "No. But if you want to put it on me…"

"I trust you," I said, frowning. "More than you trust me. But since you'll be sleeping alone in here…"

She clasped her hands together in supplication. "Please, Master, please let me sleep in your room, even if I sleep on the floor."

I held up a finger to silence her. "Where do you sleep when you've been naughty?"

Her face fell. "Alone. I sleep alone in here when I've been bad."

The welling tears almost defeated my sense of purpose. Naughty slaves slept alone. It was one of our rules, and if I made her follow the rules, I had to follow the rules too. I'd sleep with her tomorrow, and things would be right again between us. The punishment would be over, penalty paid, behavior improved. That was the way things worked.

I fitted the custom-made chastity belt onto her hips and smoothed the metal plate between her legs before cinching it snugly in the back. I turned the key in the lock and reminded her that it would be on my bedside table if she needed it. Emergencies only, of course.

I ordered her into bed and hardened myself against her sad, puppy-dog eyes. Did I want to sleep beside her? Yes. Did I want to slide into bed with her and kiss her all night while I ran my fingers over the straps and links of her chastity belt? Fuck yes, but I only tucked her covers tightly around her and kissed her on the cheek.

"All right?" I asked.

"Yes, Sir," she whispered.

"Tomorrow's a new day."

She nodded, wiping away tears. Again, I considered lifting her up and carrying her into my room, but all that would prove was that I was weak, and she needed me to be strong. I got up and left, and returned to my own empty bed, and masturbated twice in a row when I could so easily have been inside her.

But sometimes, for a punishment to be effective, you had to punish yourself too.

CHAPTER THREE:
SUBMISSION

The housekeeper made breakfast during the week, served promptly at seven. I showed up to the table to find Price bent over his tablet, and a folded piece of paper tucked beside a chocolate truffle at my plate.

He looked up and studied me, and murmured "Good morning."

"Good morning," I returned in a mostly steady voice.

A half hour ago I'd had his cock in my mouth, hard morning wood driving deep in my throat to remind me of my place, or more accurately, his ownership. Afterward he'd unlocked me from the chastity belt—that felt like ownership too—and told me to clean up and put on my clothes for work. Vera, the housekeeper, knew none of this. She only came by in the mornings to cook and straighten up, and make sure the kitchen was stocked with all of Price's favorite foods.

God, I was tired today, and sore. My feelings seemed to mill on the surface and my nerves felt stripped. Vera bustled in from the kitchen bearing omelets, fruit, kefir, and a plate of lightly buttered toast.

Price thanked her while I reached for the piece of paper and unfolded it, and held it in my lap. His dark, bold handwriting had become my compass point, my map, and sometimes my life jacket when I thought I might drown.

The sound of you, a mournful wailing,
A million Sirens, a goddess crooning
In perfect, magnificent surrender

I looked up at him as Vera left, feeling shy. "Thank you," I said.

"You're welcome."

I thought the poetry he wrote was a thousand times better than the poetry he used to give me, written by someone else. His words were as powerful as his architecture and design, to me anyway. They were as powerful as the way he touched me and controlled me, and fucked me every night. I stole glances at him as he started to eat, wondering for the millionth time how I'd gotten here, how I'd ended up in this strange, fraught relationship.

"How did you sleep?" he asked.

"Not very well. I missed you."

I noted the slight purse of his lips. "I missed you too. Now it's time to set a new goal." He put down his fork, wiped his mouth with the napkin in his lap, and looked at me. "You have two weeks from the time we return from Paris to find your first client. I want you to try harder this time, so we don't have to fucking do this again."

"Yes, Sir."

"One client will lead to another client, which will lead to another client, and so on. It's hard work, but I know you can do it. You're strong."

I loved when he called me strong. Somehow, he'd gotten it in his head that I was this scrappy little fighter, although I didn't see that in myself. I was trying to see it, for him.

Vera came in with hot coffee and we fell silent. When she left, I pushed my phone across the table to him. "Andrew and I texted last night."

Price didn't allow me to talk to men on my phone outside of work, period, and when I texted with men, even Andrew, I had to show him our conversations. It was a creepy rule, rooted in his need for control. *Did you think I was joking?* he'd snapped, the first time he asked for my phone. *Do you understand what it means to belong to me?*

We'd had a lot of those conversations in the first few days, when he'd piled rule after rule on top of me and told me I had no say in how he ran our relationship. He was in charge, I was not, and he let me know it from the start. He'd warned me, hadn't he? He'd left me, twice, because he felt he'd be a bad influence on me, too controlling and overbearing. I'd begged him to return and control me.

So that's what this was, me sitting here with a sore, hurting ass while Price scanned last night's text conversation with my gay best friend. Of course, I'd had to warn Andrew that his texts might be read, full privacy disclosure. I tried to make it sound fun and kinky, that Price insisted on having my passwords and occasionally checking my texts as a power exchange thing. "So be careful what you say," I'd warned him.

Andrew definitely found it creepy, but he was in a power exchange relationship too, subbing to his boyfriend Craig, so what could he really say? For all his lectures about red flags, I think he was secretly excited to have Price read the details of his sex life with Craig. He wasn't so happy about the no-calls-from-men rule.

So I can't ever call you? he texted when I told him why I never answered the phone.

I see you once a week. We can talk then.

At least your Lord and Master allows that.

Yes, sometimes he lets me out of the dungeon to do things, I texted back, like our thing was cute and okay.

But maybe it wasn't okay.

Price flicked through the conversation. It had been short. I hadn't been much in the mood for chatter and Andrew had just wanted to say good night. He slid the phone back to me. It was his phone, on his plan where he could check who I called and how long we talked. He'd taken away my own phone when I moved in.

Was all of this okay? I didn't know. I touched the truffle beside my plate and decided to eat it first. Milk chocolate, my favorite. I bit into the sphere of ecstasy, brushing away the cocoa shavings that fell onto the table.

"Where do you find these?" I asked. "They're orgasmic."

"They're from Switzerland. That's all I'm saying, because I don't want you running off to buy them for yourself."

"You think I'll get too fat?"

31

"No. I think they're for special occasions, like the morning after a hard punishment, to celebrate the fact that you're still here and didn't run away from me in the middle of the night."

He smiled at me, his hair so blond in the morning sun, his eyes light and shining. He looked different at the breakfast table than he looked in the dungeon, or in his dark bedroom.

"I'm still here," I said, feeling some of my tension ebb away. "Where was I going to run in that chastity belt? It only comes off with your key."

His smile widened. We both knew I could take a pair of scissors to the leather straps and have it off within a heartbeat. But I didn't, and I guessed that was why he smiled at me that way, and wrote me poems that made everything inside me glow.

"When I talked about coming here, about giving myself to you, Andrew tried to talk me out of it," I said, licking chocolate from my fingers. "I mean, not really talk me out of it, but to think about what I might have to give up. He asked what I'd do if you never let me have chocolate, or only let me have it every once in a while, as a reward for servicing your friends."

"Servicing my friends?" His smile faded.

"It was a joke," I said quickly. "Because he sees you as this scary, heartless Dom."

"Well, it's a shitty joke. I'd never share you with anyone, not for chocolate or anything else."

His hand moved on the table, toward mine, but didn't quite reach me. The serenity of moments before was gone. He seemed agitated and upset.

"Andrew's a pervert," I said, trying to diffuse the situation. "He didn't mean anything by it."

"Does he think I would do that? Loan you to people? Does Craig whore him out to his buddies?"

"No, I don't think so."

"Fuck."

He turned back to his tablet. I took that *Fuck* as the end of our conversation and started to eat. It made me happy that he got angry at the idea of sharing me, even if he wouldn't quite take my hand. Price almost never said he loved me, but there were moments like these when the depth of his love revealed itself to me like the sun from behind a gray, dark cloud.

Price got a call on his phone and muted it, then looked up at me.

"Are you excited to go to Paris?" he asked.

I swallowed a mouthful of omelet. "I've been there before."

I could have kicked myself for saying that, because the one time I'd gone to Paris I'd been with Simon, and my abusive ex-boyfriend was Price's least favorite person in the world.

"I'm excited to go again," I said, staring at my plate. "I'm older now. I'll be seeing it through different eyes."

"There are a world of things for a designer to enjoy in Paris."

There was the nudge. Paris was going to be a working holiday for us both. He'd be attending meetings at the International Symposium of Architects, and I'd be expected to go out and enrich myself.

"I wish I spoke French like you," I said.

He shrugged. "Most people there will understand English if you get in a bind. I'll give you a list of places to visit, and hire you a driver for the week."

Life was so simple when you had jillions of dollars. He was so rich, so capable. So demanding. So controlling. I touched his poem and slid him a look. He was staring back with his pale blue eyes that seemed to capture everything.

It's okay, I told myself. *Don't worry. Everything's perfectly okay.*

* * * * *

The long trip over the ocean seemed shorter with Chere along for the ride. She sat beside me in first class, sipping wine, crossing her legs every so often just to drive me insane.

We were alone this time, unlike our previous trip across the ocean to Oslo. No associates to entertain, no lustful glances to disguise as simple attention. As soon as we arrived, I took her to the downtown hotel where the conference was being held. The plane ride was foreplay. I wanted to fuck and I wanted to fuck hard. It took all my self-control to endure the obsequious welcome from the ritzy hotel's staff.

Chere, on the other hand, had stars in her eyes, so I put up with it for her, when I might otherwise have cut the welcome short. I'd grown up in

33

a life of privilege. Chere had grown up under much grimmer circumstances, and I tried to remember that at times like these. She took my hand in the elevator and squeezed it. So much glass, so much sparkle, so much rich color and plush Turkish carpets and ornate, glistening chandeliers.

"Okay?" I asked.

"This is beautiful," she whispered. "Wow. It's amazing."

I'd been with so many women who put on an act, who pretended to be swept away, but were, in reality, avaricious bitches. Chere wasn't an avaricious bitch. She was heart and soul and everything, and she was mine as long as I managed to hold on to her. I had her collar in my luggage, but our thing was about more than collars and protocols.

When we were finally alone in the room, I didn't wait to unpack her collar. I shoved her up against the wall and swallowed her shocked little *unh* with a violent kiss.

"You like it here?" I whispered.

I'd barely given her time to look around the room, but it was a classic luxury hotel room, corner, upper floor. I undressed her, being too careless and too rough. I felt something rip, but she didn't stop me or complain. We'd have it repaired later. I needed to be inside her. She tugged at my buttons, helping me take off my shirt. I yanked down my pants and pressed her to the wall with my aching, erect cock trapped between us.

She made excited little sounds, struggling against me. I reached for her neck and gripped it hard, and almost, *almost* choked her out, but this wasn't the place to do it, where she might fall and hurt herself. With a frustrated growl, I released her neck and dragged her toward the bed.

She fought in earnest now. I mean, anyone would fight in her position, with some brute trying to take away her air, especially when that brute was responsible for the lingering bruises on her ass and legs. She pulled away from me and tried to crawl across the bed. I fell on top of her and wrestled her onto her back.

"You're mine," I said, grabbing her neck again. "Submit."

She shook her head, holding my gaze. She wasn't disputing that she was mine; if she could have talked, she would have agreed with me. No, she just didn't want me to choke her. Her fingers clawed at my chest. With my other hand, I yanked one of her legs up and positioned myself between her thighs. If she really didn't want me to choke her, she should have laid still. Her squirming and panic inflamed my deepest lusts. I kissed her full lips and thrust into her wet, clenching pussy, never releasing my grip on her neck.

Her enveloping heat almost undid me. I jammed myself inside her to the hilt. "Look at me," I said. "Who do you belong to?"

"You," she rasped.

My hand tightened on her neck. She tried to pull my fingers away but I subdued her with a soft warning. "Don't fight me."

I can't explain why I had to choke her out every once in a while. I was careful. I knew how to do it so she'd be safe, but I knew she didn't like it, especially when I was actively fucking her. Maybe that was why I did it, to exert more control, the ultimate control. *I have your life. I have your breath.*

I put a finger over her pulse, exerted the necessary pressure, and watched her eyes flutter closed. Her body went slack beneath mine, her hands falling away from their death grip on my wrist. My princess, my Sleeping Beauty, out for a few seconds rather than a hundred years. I gathered her close and thrust deep so I'd be all the way inside her when she came to. She awoke with a weak, keening sound.

I cradled her against me and gentled my thrusts. "There you are," I said. "I have you. I'm inside you."

"Don't...again," she pleaded.

I hushed her. I wouldn't do it again, but she wasn't allowed to give orders either. I kissed her and squeezed her ass, still sore from her punishment a few days earlier. So many cruelties. I'd warned her before she came to stay with me. Now I couldn't let her go.

"Does that feel good, baby?" I asked as she moved her hips against mine. "You want it harder? Deeper?"

"I want you to hurt me." She clung to my shoulders. "Please, take me there..."

There. That mysterious place where both of us discarded self-preservation and inhibition and lost ourselves in the fuck. It was never hard for us to get there. Now that she seemed stronger and more lucid, I held her down and drove inside her, shuddering at the exquisite sensations in my cock, in my balls as they banged against her. She struggled against my control, reaching for her own pleasure.

I let her take it, whatever she could get. We fucked so hard we moved the bed. I could hear it scraping across the floor, but that only heightened the intensity of her surrender—and mine.

"Come now," I gasped, unable to wait any longer. "Come with me. Do it."

She always responded well to orders. I felt her clamp around my spasming organ, milking the cum out of me. Jesus, Jesus, God, *fuck*. Shudders raced up my spine. Pleasure swallowed me and spit me out on the other side of my orgasm. Or her orgasm. Our orgasm, our own creation, our "there."

"Holy fuck," I said, releasing her arms to grab her hair. I ground my cock inside her, still riding out aftershocks, and kissed her hard on the mouth. I stuck my tongue between her lips, wanting to taste her and devour her. She arched against me, squeezing her legs around my hips. We didn't talk for long moments after that, just kissed and tried to extricate ourselves from the compulsion that drew us together. I never wanted to leave her. From the first time I'd fucked her, in a similarly luxurious hotel room, I hadn't wanted to leave her.

But there were things we had to do. Unpack. Rest. Eat.

I rolled off her with a groan and lay beside her, one arm slung across my eyes. The afternoon light was fading. We'd been up early to get to the airport. Food. I wanted food.

"Are you hungry?" I asked, rolling back to pull her close.

"I'm starving."

I groped for the phone and ordered mountains of food, and then we stumbled to the shower to wash off travel grit and sex juices, and sleepiness. We put on white, fleecy hotel robes and did some cursory unpacking while we waited for the food to arrive. Chere kept stopping to stare out at the lights of the darkening city, so I drew her over to the window. We looked down together at the Rue de Rivoli, the Tuileries Garden across from the hotel, and the Eiffel Tower in the distance. "The Louvre is nearby," I said. "Maybe you can go there tomorrow."

"Maybe. Yes. That would be fun."

I tilted her head back to kiss the hollow at the base of her neck. "Thank you," I said.

"For what?"

"For being here with me."

She gave a soft laugh. "It's my pleasure to be with you. Whenever, wherever you want."

I replaced my tongue with a firm press of fingers. "Really?"

She tensed, but didn't resist. "Really," she said. "I really like being with you. I love being with you." She bit her lip, flushing, shy. Adorable. "I love you, Price."

I looked at her, wondering what to say. I loved her, yes, but that wasn't encompassing enough. She needed another poem. Maybe I could work on one tomorrow, during breaks in the symposium. A knock interrupted my awkward silence, and she started to pull away.

I yanked her back, held her neck, and pressed my forehead to hers. "I love you, starshine."

The breath she'd been holding eased out. She needed me to avow my love, so I did, but I felt so much more for her—both good and bad.

We sat and ate together in a half-dark hotel room looking out at the Paris lights, and then fell into bed, sexually and gastronomically spent. We shed the robes and slid under the sheets, too exhausted to kiss or fuck or do anything but drift to oblivion in each other's arms. Tomorrow, we'd conquer the city. Tonight, we needed sleep.

CHAPTER FOUR:
PARIS

I woke to Price pressed against my back, his cock pushing inside me. I stretched and arched within his muscular grasp. His stubbled cheeks pricked me as he kissed my neck, then closed his teeth on my earlobe.

"Ow," I said drowsily. "No biting."

"Don't tell me what to do," he said, but his bite gentled to a nibble. I looked back over my shoulder in the gray morning light, holding his gaze as he slid deeper inside me. His eyes were so blue, so intent even in the dim hotel room.

"Paris makes me horny," he said through his teeth.

"Oh. Good." His fingers roved over my body, touching all my sensitive spots, all my curves. One of his hands eventually found its way to my neck, but unlike last night, he didn't grip me. He stroked over my pulse instead. I squirmed and squeezed on his cock as my pussy came to life. I arched for more. *Oh yes, yeah, please, my G-spot...*

He held my hips, stilling my movements. "Don't be a mindless little slut," he chided. "Or I might not let you come."

I whined and felt his smile against my cheek. I loved when he was playful, when we had close, affectionate encounters under the covers before we got up. He pressed inside me again, so, so slow, holding my hips so I couldn't bounce back against him the way I wanted to. I arched so my shoulder blades rubbed against his chest.

"I guess Paris makes you horny too, little slave girl."

Little slave girl. *Yes, I'm your slave. Yes, you make me so horny and excited.* He let go of my hips and circled my waist, holding me against him. Even when he was slow and sensual, he maintained control. I loved it. Without that control, I would have been lost.

"Oh, please," I said, writhing against his hard muscles as he entered me again.

He waited inside me, scratching my cheek and jaw with a series of fleeting kisses. "You want more?" he asked.

"Yes, Sir, I want more." I knew my part in this erotic drama. "Please, give me more."

"Tell me what you want. You want it in another hole?" I sighed as he squeezed my ass cheeks, parting them, teasing me with a threat. "You want me in your tight little asshole?"

"Yes, Sir, I would love that," I breathed.

"It might hurt. Do you want me to hurt you?"

"I always want you to hurt me." That was the goddamn truth. Since we'd started this dirty negotiation, my pussy had grown ten times wetter.

"Ask for it," he said. "Ask for what you want."

"Please fuck my ass. I want to feel your big, thick cock inside my tight asshole."

"I bet you fucking do." He leaned away. The bed shifted, and he got up. "Don't move. You stay right there."

He didn't have to tell me. I waited on my side for him to return with the lube. His cock was massively hard, bouncing with each step as he came back to me. He slathered lube over the reddened crown, more than he used when I was a bad girl. I appreciated that he added a little extra to my asshole. My mind was willing—no, eager—for some snuggle anal, but my body was still half-asleep.

He slid closer to me, easing his cock between my ass cheeks. He pressed on my hole, forcing his way forward. I could feel his fingers against my ass, and then it was just his thick shaft sliding inside me, eased by the extra lube.

Oh God, it hurt. Of course it always hurt when something that big was forced into a place that small, but it hurt in the most wonderful way possible, because his arms slid around me again and held me close. His stubble scraped the back of my neck as I curled into the pain. His big hands opened against my heart, then one slid up to my neck again. No choking. Just holding. There was no need to subjugate me beyond the firm, steady strokes invading my ass.

"Is that better?" he said against my ear. "Is that what you needed?"

"Yes, Sir. Thank you. Oh God, thank you."

I added the last thank you because his other caressing hand had found its way down to my clit. He parted me, sliding a fingertip over my throbbing button. I clenched so hard around his cock that he gasped. He slid his hand lower and shoved his fingers into my pussy, filling the space he'd left empty when he decided to fuck my ass. My toes curled with happiness. He had big fucking fingers and he knew how to use them.

"Oh my God, oh my God, oh my God," I babbled.

"Does that feel good?"

"Oh God."

"I'll take that as a yes." He shoved his fingers deeper. "Horny little girl. Do you like feeling all filled up?"

With Price in my life, it was hard to avoid that feeling. He was inside me and around me all the time, and I'd become scarily addicted to his nearness, to the *fullness* of his mastery.

He pressed my clit with the heel of his hand as he fingerfucked me, and continued drilling my ass. I was glad Paris made him horny. I clung to his arms, climbing toward orgasm. "Please, please," I whispered. I meant *Please don't stop. Please let me come.*

He pressed against me, all down my back and thighs, like he wanted to become part of me. But he was already part of me, more than anyone else had been.

Please, please, please…

"Come," he said. Not *Are you going to come?* Or *I want you to come.* Just the simple command. *Come.* He slid deep inside my ass and stayed there, allowing me to jerk off on his fingers while I was impaled. I felt warm, safe, and of course, deliciously filled up. The orgasm unfolded like the best morning orgasms, in a shatteringly intense rumble of sensation. The earthquake started in my pussy and ass, then reverberated out to the rest of my body, until my nipples were aching and my toes were once again curled in ecstasy.

It was a long time before I uncurled them. I felt him shuddering at my back, stifling the roar that sometimes accompanied his orgasms. This was too close and snuggly for that. Instead I got another volley of kisses along my neck, and another hard bite on my ear.

"Ow," I said, even though I barely felt it. My pussy was still contracting around his fingers, and my ass still felt full. I sighed when he finally pulled away.

"That was wonderful," I whispered.

"Wonderful and naughty."

I turned and nestled against his chest. "You make me so naughty."

He laughed. "I think you were plenty naughty before I came along. I just know how to capitalize on your filthy urges."

"*My* filthy urges?" I feigned outrage. "You suggested anal."

"Silence, filthy little slave."

He prevented further outbursts by sticking his tongue in my mouth and kissing me into submission. By the end of our make out session, I felt so blissed out and content I could have fallen back to sleep, but he wouldn't allow that. After a shower and an elegant breakfast in the restaurant downstairs, I headed out into Paris determined to wring all the inspiration I could from the City of Love. While Price attended his conference, I was to spend my day exploring the Louvre.

Honestly, I could have spent a month at the Louvre absorbing everything I wanted to see. I made a list of each exhibit I visited, because I knew Price would ask me about them when he returned to the hotel. I took a break at lunchtime and basked in the sun at an outdoor cafe. So many people, some locals, some tourists. It struck me that they all had a story, perhaps as complicated and disjointed as my own. As traumatic as my own.

No, I didn't want to think about that here, in the sun and loveliness of Paris. My past was my past. I knew that, but it still haunted me sometimes. Here in Paris, the past felt very close. I couldn't help remembering the time I'd come here with Simon, and walked with him through the Louvre until we found his newly installed painting. *Heart-Lust.* I could close my eyes and see it, or...

Well, I was here at the Louvre. I could go see it for real.

But I couldn't. I shouldn't. After our run in with Simon at Andrew's art show, Price had forbidden me to have anything to do with my ex.

He'd actually forbidden it two years earlier, when he'd bought me an apartment on the condition that Simon never set foot inside.

Still, the painting wasn't Simon. It wasn't like I was drifting toward the Modern Impressionists area of the museum so I could see Simon.

It's your history with him, my conscience whispered. *It's practically the same.*

I tried to get engrossed in other things, but I kept thinking of *Heart-Lust* as Simon had worked on it, as it had hung on his studio wall in our loft. He'd done other paintings inspired by me, but that was the first one, the one that changed my life.

I thought of how he'd stood me in front of it and pointed out all the things I couldn't see in the whirls and swirls of scarlet paint. I thought of the poem Simon had given me. *Her heart breaks in a smile, and she is lust.* It was the same E.E. Cummings poem that Price had given me years later when my life—and my relationship with Simon—was falling apart. In that way, *Heart-Lust* joined all of our histories, and I was here in Paris, so why shouldn't I see it while I had the chance?

Because Price wouldn't want you to...

I silenced the warning in my head and found my way to the correct gallery. I tried to go by memory, but in the end I had to consult a map. Funny how we forget things we should remember so intensely, or perhaps the museum itself had changed.

But when I found the right place and walked into the large atrium where the painting was lit and mounted, I was shaken by a recognition so strong and so poignant that my eyes filled with tears.

Heart-Lust. It was a beautiful mess, just like Simon had been before he got sober, just like I was before I met Price. The massive, rough-edged canvas was red and angry and sweet and lyrical at once.

I was over Simon, I was absolutely over him, but the sadness of our ten-year failed relationship would always be there, just like this painting would always be on display in the world. On the back, where no one could see, he'd painted my name over and over, *Chere Chere Chere Chere Chere.* I couldn't see that now. I couldn't touch it the way I once had, with Simon's permission. I couldn't run my fingers over the textures, not with the surly museum docent standing in the corner. *But I did it once,* I thought. *I traced those million dollar brush strokes. I have quite a contemptible past.*

Price hated when I lived in the past. He'd be angry to know I was lingering here, staring at *Heart-Lust*, crying and reminiscing over a relationship that had been so very bad. I'd have to confess that I'd visited Simon's painting. He'd consider it a breach of the rules. He'd punish me. *This isn't why you're in Paris.* I could practically hear him say it in his hard, firm, angry-Master voice. He'd tell me that I needed to look forward, not back. I needed to become who I was supposed to be.

I turned to escape this wing, wiping away guilty tears. I had my head down, so I didn't see the elderly man I bumped into. A younger man at his side steadied him with a sharp, foreign volley of words.

"I'm so sorry," I stammered, looking into dark silver eyes framed by thinning gray hair. The old man had deeply bronzed skin and a compact body that felt strong for his age. His companion watched me with dark eyes, inclining his own head of jet black, close-cropped hair.

"Are you all right?" the older man asked. "Our collision was my fault. I was fiddling with my tie pin."

His English was impeccable, despite his Indian accent. His clothing, for that matter, was impeccable. Rich suit, rich shoes, and a jewel-encrusted gold tie pin that was indeed sagging to one side.

"It's a bit top-heavy for a tie pin," I said, as he fussed at it some more.

"I know, and it greatly disappoints me. I had it specially made."

The giant at his side muttered something urgent, but the gray-haired businessman waved a hand.

"She's not going to steal anything," he said. "She is not a gypsy. She speaks English." His striking silver eyes softened as they studied me. "She is a lover of art. Look, she's been crying."

I ran fingers beneath my eyes. "These paintings are so powerful," I said, even though I was really crying about something else. "I'm sorry I bumped into you."

"My dear, I am a lover of art as well. I understand how it can affect you. My name is Vinod, and this is my friend Jino, who follows me about to make sure I don't get into trouble."

I took his hand when he offered it. His fingers felt soft and cool. Though his "friend" was very tall, the old man was just my height, so it was easy to hold his gaze.

"I'm Chere. It's nice to meet you." I looked back at his tie pin, wishing I could take it off and try to fix it. "I design jewelry," I said. "Forgive me, but I think that piece is poorly made, even if it's beautiful."

He gave a grunt of agreement. "You see," he said, turning to his companion. "Finally, some honesty." He plucked at the pin again. "They say it's my fault, that I don't position it properly. But no matter how I position the thing, it droops."

"I think maybe...it's just too much. I could take that apart and make three different tie pins that were just as beautiful with less weight. Right now..." I touched the heavy piece. "Right now it has too much all at once. Sometimes understated elegance looks just as rich."

"You say you're a designer?" he asked, regarding me closely. "Do you have a studio here in Paris?"

"I have one in New York, on Park Avenue." I was trying to sound more important than I was, like I had some big storefront when all I had was a two-room converted office. Still... "Can I give you my card? Or..." I slid a look at his companion, who I had come to suspect was a bodyguard. "I'm staying at a hotel just down the street. I have some samples with me, tie pins and cuff links and women's jewelry too. I also do custom work, if you..." *If you would like to become a client. You obviously have money, and I don't want to get my ass beaten...again...*

"I would like to learn more about your aesthetic," he said. "I love anything well-executed, and lately understated elegance has been in short supply."

We returned to the hotel in the car Price had hired for me, keeping up a steady stream of conversation. Vinod was excited when he learned I'd recently graduated from the Norton School of Art and Design, and told me a little about his work in a fashion design firm in Mumbai. We were on the elevator heading upstairs before I realized I didn't really know these two men. I'd been so excited that someone was interested in my work that I hadn't considered whether it was safe or reasonable to invite them to my room. It wasn't even my room, it was Price's room.

But in my ten years as an escort I'd developed a sixth sense about people, and Vinod didn't have a shred of evil about him. This might be my only chance to pick up a client, so I decided it was worth the risk.

When I keyed into the room, Vinod didn't even react to the grandeur of the furnishings and the breathtaking view. He exuded wealthy privilege.

He must be so rich. I took out the small case of samples I'd brought just in case an opportunity like this arose. Jino lingered a few feet away, but Vinod leaned over the array of delicate pieces and took them in with an avid gaze.

"Yes, I see what you mean," he said in his clipped accent. "These are simple but beautiful. Elegance defined."

"I've always believed less is more." I dug for a tie pin half the size of his, made of smooth polished silver with one dark pearl set into the tip. "Try this. It'll look great with the color of your coat."

Vinod took off his pin and handed it to Jino, and slid my pin into the smooth black silk of his tie. It wasn't an everyday look. It looked fancy, even regal, but it fit Vinod's style.

"There are matching cuff links," I said, fishing them out. "And a ring."

"How beautiful these are. You made them?"

"I make everything."

"Why haven't you been snapped up by some big fashion house?" he asked, his brows coming together in a dark line. "This is inspired design. So novel, so simple, and yet so striking." He fiddled with the cuff links and finally held out his wrists so I could help him. That was when the door beeped and clicked, and Price walked in.

He stopped just inside, taking in Jino first, and then Vinod. I saw a flash of anger, then a rueful scowl as he crossed his arms over his chest. I was putting together the words to explain how I'd met them and why they were here, when Vinod walked to Price and greeted him by name.

"Ah, Mr. Eriksen. Of course this little visionary belongs to you."

"Yes, that one's mine," he said. "What a pleasure to see you again, Mr. Sushil."

"The pleasure is mine. Are you in town for the architecture conference?"

Price nodded, looking between the two of us. Jino had gone to sit on the couch. "I have to admit," said Price, "you're the last person I expected to find in my hotel room. What are you doing here? How do you know Chere?"

"I found her in the Modern Impressionists wing." Vinod looked at me fondly. "She was in tears over something she'd encountered there, so I couldn't fault her for barging into me, even if she almost knocked me down."

Price's gaze met mine. Maybe I looked guilty, or maybe he just *knew*. He wasn't an idiot. He knew Simon's painting was in the Louvre, and that he was a modern impressionist. It was all I could do not to flinch under his prolonged regard. Meanwhile, Vinod continued relating the story of our collision in the museum, and his travails with his tie pin, and how I'd come to the rescue with my "ground breaking designs."

Come to his rescue? Ground breaking designs?

I stood like someone lost in a dream as he showed Price the cuff links he'd tried on, and the ring. Price showed Vinod his cuff links, also of my design. The Indian man clapped a hand against his heart and said, "She is so raw. So fresh. We need an eye like this. We need designs like this."

"You need them for whom?" I asked.

"For whom?" Vinod made an expansive gesture. "For everyone, my dear. For the entire world."

"Vinod," said Price. "Would you and Jino care to join us for dinner? I'd love to catch up."

* * * * *

Only Chere could go to a cavernous French museum, bewitch an eccentric multi-billionaire by almost knocking him over, and then invite him back to our room without even knowing who the fuck he was.

Vinod Sushil was an Indian fashion magnate, overseeing hundreds of brands and boutiques throughout central Asia and the Far East. I knew him from my time in Mumbai, from years of contact within the Indian design community. We'd spoken together at decadent parties and glittering charity events. He'd been there when they'd opened my bridge, congratulating me on the culmination of a three-year project.

I'd told her to pick up a client, one client, to avoid further punishment. Instead she'd tapped into half the world's fashion market by charming an old man at the Louvre. In the *Modern Impressionists wing*, damn her. Vinod believed she was sensitive and artistic because he'd found her in tears, but I was pretty sure I knew the real reason she'd been in tears.

46

And yes, I felt sorry for her. She'd survived a hell of a depressing relationship with Simon, a ten-year slide into codependence and self-loathing. But if that was the case, why had she gone to see his painting? Why had she gotten emotional over it? Did she still feel something for Simon? Had she forgotten how terrible things had been while they were together?

I watched her during dinner, trying to gauge her thoughts. My own thoughts cycled between disappointment, suspicion, and unbridled fury. Simon Baldwin was an asshole, and I...

Well, I was better than him. I knew I was better than him, that I treated her with more kindness and respect. Didn't I?

Maybe she didn't see it that way. Maybe my level of control was too much. But I'd warned her. Maybe she was tired of the sex. We had so much sex, until I thought I probably exhausted her. She and Simon never had sex at the end. Maybe she'd prefer that.

Ugh, I had to get out of my head. I took another sip of wine and tried to follow Chere and Vinod's animated conversation. Jino sat to Vinod's side, a stone-faced gargoyle whose partnership with his employer was a much-discussed controversy. The two of them denied their relationship was anything but professional, but there was something in the way Jino watched over him that went beyond dutiful vigilance.

That's how I felt toward Chere. It went beyond dutiful vigilance to possession and proprietary demands. I reluctantly agreed that Chere could spend more time with Vinod while we were in Paris, to talk about design and collaboration. I'd had other plans for her time here, carefully considered plans that she would now have to break. It felt like a loss of control.

But you can't harm her. You can't suffocate her. You have to let her grow.

I feared that she'd grow so much she'd drift away from me. I had so many fears. I was a ridiculous, fear-riddled man, and dinner was hard as fuck for me to cope with, and Vinod's effusive estimation of her talent was hard for me to cope with, and her smiles for him were hard to cope with even if he was seventy fucking years old and reputed to be gay, and why the hell had she cried over Simon's painting? Why had she visited it at all?

By the time we parted with Vinod and Jino and returned to our hotel room, everything seemed alarmingly unstable and fucked up. I felt confused about what to do, and Chere was nervous and overexcited, and we had to have a discussion that was going to get pretty brutal by the end, because it was about Simon and her, and her checkered past, and our past, which wasn't exactly a fairy tale either. Fuck.

"Take off your clothes and sit on the bed," I said, pointing to the spot where I wanted her to plant her ass.

She murmured something. Maybe *Yes, Sir*. She was immediately on guard, which only underlined the fact that we had tough shit to talk about. I watched her undress and fold her clothes with shaking fingers. When she was done, and sitting where I'd told her, I stood in front of her and buckled her collar around her neck.

"How was the Louvre today?" I asked. "Aside from meeting Vinod Sushil?"

"It was good. Nice."

"Nice?" I grimaced and stepped back from her, crossing my arms over my chest. "What did you see while you were there?"

She let out a soft, slow breath and looked up at me. "I saw a lot of things. I did what you asked. I spent the day there looking for inspiration."

"Did you find it?"

"I found a customer. Vinod's interested in producing some of my designs for his spring lines." Her chin lifted a little. Her fingers glanced over her collar before returning to her lap. "That's what you told me to do. I did everything you told me to do."

"And something you knew you weren't allowed to do." She paled at my sharp voice. Her lips tightened. If I'd had any lingering doubt of what she'd done, or why Vinod found her in tears in the Modern Impressionist area, her guilty expression washed those doubts away. "Confess it," I said. "Don't play games with me."

Tears rose in her eyes. "Today of all days, I thought you'd be happy."

"I'm happy about some things. Not so happy about others. Say it. Tell me what you did."

"I went to see Simon's painting," she said in a rebellious tone. "I don't get to Paris that often, and it was right there—"

"I don't care to hear your excuses. Who do you belong to?"

"You." Her voice trembled on the word. Maybe I was being too scary. I felt a scary intense love for her, even though she'd disappointed me.

"You belong to me," I agreed after a heavy silence. "And what is my rule about Simon?"

"I hate when you do this."

"Do what? Hold you accountable for the rules you agreed to follow?" I hooked a finger through her collar's O-ring and gave her a shake. "Do you want to take this off? Are you done with me?"

The tears that swam in her eyes welled over and fell as she shook her head. "No, Sir. Of course not. It's just...he made that painting for me."

She looked very sorry, and very guilty. "Sit up straight," I said, not willing to let her cry her way out of this.

"I'm sorry I went to see it. I should have asked your permission first."

"I would have said no. Did you enjoy seeing it?" I looked at her hard. "Was it worth getting punished over? You're to have no contact with Simon Baldwin. None. Zero."

"I know. It was just...the history of it."

"What history? The history when he abused you? When he used you and pimped you out so he could get high?"

"He's sober now."

"I know he's fucking sober." *Wrong thing to say, Chere. Wrong thing to do, defending your bastard ex.*

"I made that rule for a reason," I said out loud. "How long were you in a relationship with Simon?"

"Ten years."

"How many times did you try to convince yourself you had to leave him?"

She put her head in her hands. I yanked her face back up and glared at her until she squeaked out an answer.

"Hundreds of times. More times than I can count."

"You are *not to have anything to do with him.*" I drew out each word in icy emphasis. "Nothing to do with him ever. No thoughts, no memories, no fucking contact whatsoever. Is that or is that not the rule?"

"It's the rule, Sir."

"I made that rule for you, Chere. For your well-being. Your sanity. Now I'm pissed off for three fucking reasons, and I'm going to tell you what they are before I bend you over and punish your ass. One: You disobeyed me. That's the first thing, that you allowed it to happen in the first place. Two: I had to drag it out of you, when you should have admitted what you did right away, as soon as we were alone together. Three..."

I paused, honing my own fearsome pain. She held my gaze, and I let her have it. "Three, Chere: You cried for him. You cried for that motherfucking asshole who brought you nothing but misery. *You cried for him.*"

"I cried for the painting," she burst out, interrupting me, challenging my authority. "I cried because I remembered when he painted it, and who I was then."

"You cried for what you had with him," I accused. "You should be happy he's out of your life."

"I am!"

"I did that, damn you. I helped you get away from him. If I hadn't, you'd probably still be in that loft, going out to turn tricks so he could shoot your dirty money through his veins or snort it up his nose."

"Dirty money?" she sobbed. "Some of that was your money. A lot of it!"

"Don't fucking remind me."

I walked away from her, preserving an adequate distance between us. I wasn't going to punish her in anger. Hurt, yes. Anger, no. I looked out the window, collecting my thoughts. Remembering *why*, as she sat very still on the bed. *It's because I love you. Because I only ever wanted to protect you.*

"I make these rules for a reason," I said, when I felt calmer. "Simon is out of your life for a reason."

"I know, Sir." She'd calmed too. Her voice sounded steadier. "I knew you'd be angry. I did it anyway. I don't have any excuse except that I wanted to do it."

"You have to listen to me," I said, turning back to her. "You have to obey my rules or none of this works."

"Yes, Sir. I know."

"You're going to be punished for what you did."

"Yes, Sir," she repeated, clenching her hands in her lap. "I know."

CHAPTER FIVE: REGRETS

I prayed for the belt. I could deal with his belt, but belts were so loud and this was a hotel room. Instead he went to his luggage and took out a whip, a long, thin, braided implement that whistled when it moved through the air, but was nearly silent on impact.

I already hurt. Oh shit, that whip was torture, and he was in a really bad mood. *This is your fault, Chere. You knew he would punish you.* Yes, I knew, but now it was happening and I was fucking terrified.

It wasn't just the terror making me shake. It was the crazy jumble of emotions from this crazy jumble of a day. Sadness over my past, guilt over the painting, joy over my new business prospects with Vinod. I literally had so many feelings I couldn't process them, and now there was this terror and regret, and the agony of seeing Price's displeasure in his hard features and ice blue eyes.

I opened my mouth to say I was sorry, or maybe plead for mercy, but his gaze silenced me. We weren't in his dungeon, but we might as well have been, and I wasn't allowed to talk there unless I was asked a question. I'd broken enough rules for today so I bit my lip to keep my pleading inside. I just had to survive this. Maybe this punishment would be good for me. Maybe it would calm all the untamed emotions crowding my brain.

Price came toward me with the whip. I was naked, so naked, while he was still dressed. He piled some pillows in the center of the bed.

"Bend over and get your ass in the air," he ordered.

The whip twitched in his hand. I did as he asked, too scared to make any response like "Yes, Sir" or "As you wish, Sir." I just bent over the pillows, pressed my knees together, and buried my head in my arms.

"Ass up," he said, louder and firmer. "Part your legs for balance. Don't you dare flop around."

I inched my legs apart and braced myself. A whimper of fear escaped my throat. I hated the whip. I had nightmares about it. It burned like liquid fire.

"You're getting thirty," he said. "Ten for going to see the painting, ten for making excuses about it, and ten for romanticizing your fucking history with him. It's *past*, Chere. Do you understand that?"

"Yes, Sir," I whispered from between my arms. Thirty? I would die from thirty, at least with that whip.

"You're getting all thirty at once," he continued. "No warm up. No breaks. You blatantly broke a fucking rule." He traced the whip across my ass, a gentle caress and poisonous mindfuckery at once. "I don't want a fucking sound. Not one sound. You earned this, and you're going to take it without moving or complaining."

I didn't think I'd be able to do that. What would he do to me when I let out a scream? Seeing the painting wasn't worth this. Simon wasn't worth this. I was a crouching, cringing huddle of regret. He stood back and I held my breath as the whip-fire barrage began. One liquid, searing line bloomed across my ass, then another, then another, so quickly one after the other that I couldn't recover between them.

I used every fiber of my strength to kneel there and take it. I wasn't perfect. I jerked with every blow and clenched my ass. Before he was ten strokes in, I'd collapsed on the pillows, but I didn't roll into a ball or try to run away. I wasn't inhuman, after all. I wasn't a robot who could take a whipping without reacting to the pain. I grabbed handfuls of the sheets to keep from reaching behind me, and shoved those handfuls between my lips to muffle my frantic sounds of distress.

Don't scream. Don't scream. I didn't scream. Thirty. Oh my God, thirty. What number was he on? My ass was a network of throbbing, aching lines and there was always more, more, more to take. I started shaking with the effort to be still, to endure. I stopped trying to muffle my cries and bit down on the sheets instead, gnashing them between my teeth. I bit down so hard, my jaw hurt. *Please, please, please.*

The entire ordeal probably lasted less than two minutes, but in those two minutes, I felt like I died, like there could never be any pain this bad, or any way to survive holding myself still. When he finished, I continued shaking. I couldn't move, not even to escape him if he started up again. I'd worked so hard at submitting to his punishment that my body was now frozen in place as an act of will.

He moved to put the whip in his luggage, then he was back, kneeling behind me on the bed. I heard his zipper, heard the sound of him shoving down his pants. I heard the cap from the lube, and I knew he'd be stingy with it. He parted my ass cheeks to lube up my hole. I flinched as his fingers squeezed my tortured flesh, and bit hard on the sheets to keep from wailing out loud.

He positioned his cock against my ass and eased the head inside me with firm, forward pressure. Tears rose in my eyes, tears I'd been too panicked to shed earlier. Now they overflowed, soaking the sheets as he pried me open with no attention to my discomfort.

Ow, ow, ow, it hurt. It was scary to be forced this way without any mental prep time. More panic noises choked out of my throat as I gripped the sheets and tried to stay open. I heard him shrug out of his shirt, but his pants were still bunched up at his knees, against my trembling legs. This wasn't romantic and sensual, like this morning. This wasn't sex. It was punishment.

And I'd known it was coming, pardon the pun. Bad girls didn't get it in the pussy. Sometimes, when it came to Price, even good girls didn't get it in the pussy, but bad girls...bad girls always got fucked in the ass so it hurt.

I clenched my toes, but kept my legs apart so he wouldn't spank me for resisting him. I wondered if he'd drawn blood with the whip. It always felt like he was skinning me alive, but then I'd look later and there'd be no broken skin at all, just a lattice of welts to remind me that I belonged to someone who believed in strictly enforced rules.

Ow, my ass. He was taking his time on the way to orgasm. He'd drive inside me slow, prying me open, then pound me as hard and deep as he could go. I wouldn't be permitted to orgasm, of course, but he would come in his own sweet time, usually when I couldn't bear to have his cock inside my ass one second longer. *You deserve this. You asked for this.*

You wanted this.

You begged to belong to him.

I pressed the balled up sheets to my eyes as he pummeled into me. He put his hands on my shoulders, pushing me down and fucking me even harder than before. My hips bumped against the pillows. I didn't dare resist him, no matter how hard he drilled me. My job was to take it like a bad, sorry girl who understood why she was being punished, who *wanted* to be punished. I tried to feel that way, but *ow...*

Finally, after what seemed like an eternity, his strokes lengthened. He drove deep, making sure I felt every inch before he got off. He moved one of his hands from my shoulder to my neck, and clutched my windpipe in a commanding grip.

"Who do you belong to?" he asked.

I gasped for air. "You, Sir."

There was no way to deny it. He was so deep and hard inside me I couldn't move. His fingers circled my collar, reminding me who I was. What I was. What I'd agreed to when he first buckled it around my neck.

"Are you sorry for what you did?" he asked, squeezing tighter.

I nodded. It was all I could do.

"Are you going to be a good girl for the rest of this fucking trip?"

I nodded again, as hard as I could with my flagging lucidity and breath.

Please, I wanted to beg. *Please...* But no begging was allowed. He finished inside me with a series of violent thrusts that slid me across the pillows. I hung onto the sheets until he came to rest. Jesus, I'd torn the bed apart. I hoped he wasn't angry. God, I didn't want him to be angry with me anymore.

He collapsed on top of me and I lay there regaining my breath and my composure, although a few tears still leaked from my eyes. I felt uncomfortably aroused from my clit being banged against the pillows so many times, but there was nothing I could do about it but lie there and endure the lingering presence of his cock. My ass felt steamed. My whole body felt hot and wrung out. He pulled away, leaving me empty.

"Let go," he said, tugging at the sheets. I realized I still held them in a death grip. He pried my fingers away when I couldn't open them of my own accord, then sat beside me, rubbing my sore ass cheeks. At some point, his pants had been kicked onto the floor. His caresses hurt, as I'm sure he meant them to. Finally, he spanked me on both cheeks—*ow! ow!*— and rolled from the bed.

"Don't move," he said. "Stay right there. I'll tell you when you can get up."

I buried my head in my arms again, feeling shamed and humiliated as he went to the table and opened his laptop, and started to work. Checking files? Answering emails? I didn't know, because I was half-lying and half-kneeling on the bed with my destroyed ass utterly exposed to his scrutiny.

Was it worth getting punished over? he'd asked me.

I didn't even have to think about it. The answer was no.

* * * * *

I left her there to wallow in her guilty shame, because it was good for her, and because it aroused me to see her kneeling in chastened defeat. Her beautiful, round ass was covered in the marks I'd given her, and her hole was fresh from a primal punishment reaming. All of it aroused me, but what turned me on most was her surrender to my will.

Even now, she'd gone back to clutching the sheets. This wasn't easy for her, not the pain, not the guilt, not the humiliation, but she put up with it because that was the price of being with me. I'd grasped her collar and asked *Are you done with me?* And my lovely slave had burst into tears and said *No, Sir. Of course not.*

Of course not, Chere. Of course we'll never be done with each other. Even after you've had enough of this pain and you finally, wisely, leave me, I'll still love you. I'll still remember these times when you gave everything to me and let me bask in it afterward, staring at your hurting, exposed body.

I wondered what she was thinking as I watched her relax by slow degrees. Very slow degrees. Had she come to some place of peace with what she'd done, and what I'd done, and this fucked up dynamic between us that was probably just as bad for her as her relationship with Simon?

No, it wasn't as bad. He hadn't loved her, and I loved her. He hadn't protected her, and I protected her from whatever I could, even if my methods were questionable or suffocating.

Are you done with me?

No, Sir. Of course not.

After too long a time, I went over and rubbed her back, and squeezed her welted ass again. I knew it hurt her, but I couldn't resist, and she was sub-spacey, floating in the peace that eluded her while the punishment was going on. I helped her from the bed and ran a bath for us, and soaked with her in the tub, to the scented pleasure of the hotel's artisanal soaps. I left her collar draped over the side, a memory and a reminder. There were no words to say, no big rehashing or lectures. The punishment was over. Now it was just her warm skin against mine, and her cheek resting against my chest.

Afterward, I put the sheets and pillows to rights while she dried off, and then we crawled into bed together. At home, I would have made her sleep in another room to complete her punishment, but here, in this busy, foreign hotel, I wanted her at my side.

I held her close and thought *Mine, you're mine. Mine, mine, mine.* I'd thought that as I whipped her. I'd thought it as I buried myself in her ass and squeezed her neck. Tomorrow, maybe, I'd be gentle with her, just a little bit gentle. She might enjoy it. I might enjoy it for as long as the feeling lasted. No matter how gentle I tried to be, we always ended up in a fever pitch.

"Price?"

Her soft voice was a magic spell in the darkness.

"Price?" she asked again. "Are you awake?"

"Yes."

"Can I tell you something? Something about what happened today?"

"Yes."

I heard a soft sigh. "I wanted to tell you I'm sorry. I don't feel anything for Simon anymore, I swear. Today was just...archaeology."

I rested my chin on her hair. "I know. It's still dangerous." I twisted one of her curls around my finger. "You remember how it was. Your past..."

"I hated my past," she whispered, so low I could barely hear her. "I wish I could erase my entire history."

I knew she felt that way, and I'd thrown it in her face anyway. I'd done it to hurt her as much as she hurt me. Sometimes sadists sucked.

"Chere, I'm sorry about..." My throat went tight. I wasn't one for apologies. "I'm sorry I said that about your dirty money. That was shitty of me. Hypocritical."

She gave a quiet, hurting laugh, which made me feel shittier, which was exactly what I deserved. "Well, you just told the truth, right?"

"Your past is your past." My voice had turned gruff. "I don't blame you for your past, but I have a problem with you romanticizing it. Longing for it."

"I don't long for it. I cried today because I felt sad. The memories are sad. The regrets..."

"We all have regrets."

Jesus, I had a million regrets. Everything before Chere was a series of regrets. If she left... I couldn't imagine the regrets I'd wrestle with then. *I don't want you to leave. Mine, mine, mine. I want you in my dungeon, my captive in a tower. Don't leave.*

"What do you regret?" she asked, snuggling closer to me. "Your life seems perfect."

That comment proved how little she knew me. I supposed that was my fault. I hadn't exactly let her into my heart, even if I'd let her into my life. From the outside, I must have seemed like the luckiest man alive, the richest, the most successful.

"I regret that I waited so long to help you when you were with Simon," I said. "That's one regret I'll live with forever."

She made a dismissive sound and slid her arms around my neck. "Don't have regrets about that. Everything you did afterward should cancel them out."

Everything I'd done afterward? Like the possessiveness? The overbearing rules? The punishment anal? The humiliation for my own pleasure?

"Someday you're going to figure out what an asshole I am," I said.

She laughed, but I wasn't joking. I slid my fingers down over her welted ass cheeks. Even in the darkness, I could make out the pattern of whip marks by feel.

"I'm proud of you." I leaned closer to her, pressing my lips to her temple and the soft line of her hair. "I'm proud that you found a client, even if it only happened because you broke a rule. Sometimes shit works out that way. Sometimes bad things turn into good things."

"I think that's true," she said after a moment. Maybe she was remembering our first session at the W Hotel, which was bad and crazy and definitely sketchy in the area of consent. I'd still enjoyed it, and she had too, and here we were. Sometimes awful things could turn into wonderful things.

Unfortunately, the opposite was also possible. Sometimes wonderful things could turn wrong and bad.

CHAPTER SIX: CLARITY

Chere rarely sulked, but there was always that time after a hard punishment when things felt tense between us. She spent the next couple days partly with Vinod and partly in the museums and artistic quarters of Paris, while I languished in conference meetings. I say I languished, but the truth was, I lived for international architecture, and appreciated the privilege of sitting on these panels and discussing ways to beautify the world. I attended this conference annually, but this year, Chere was with me and I missed her.

It wasn't only the sex, although I fucking loved the sex. No, it was some part of me that relaxed and unwound when she was near me. To put it simply: she made me happy. My past relationships had been full of anger and artifice, and disgust with everything to do with love. How did I feel about love now? Jesus.

Fuck.

The conference ended on Friday, but we didn't fly out right away. I'd arranged a little extra time so we could walk around Paris together. Why not? We'd had so much fun exploring Oslo earlier in the year.

We spent the first part of our free day in bed, grasping one another, fucking, struggling, kissing. Faint welts lingered on Chere's ass, but the post-punishment distance between us had mostly melted.

It was tempting to remain in bed, but she was happy and bright, and excited to walk around the city with me instead of being on her own. She was thrilled to spend time with me, an emotional shock I never got used to. She liked me, sadism and all. She *loved* me.

I took off her collar and we left the hotel to stroll through the Tuileries Garden. Like so many things in Paris, the sculptures and statues were enough to make any designer's head spin. Green lawn, fountains, flowers, and stately lines of trees...there were so many things to look at, and so many people.

Chere didn't point out the broad motifs—the grand circles and intricately planned walkways. No, as always she was drawn to things ninety-nine percent of people never noticed, things like minute etchings on the statues, or the berry bushes that were just starting to turn orange for fall. Orange was my least favorite color, but she made it seem beautiful.

"Does this inspire you?" I asked as we gazed across the grounds.

"Yes," she said. "But it's so busy here."

I could take a hint. We left the Tuileries to explore some of Paris's quieter streets, hidden avenues with narrow shop fronts and historical architecture. We proceeded at a snail's pace, her avid eyes taking in everything as I attempted to teach her some French. Her accent was awful as she ordered our lunch at a corner bistro. I asked for wine, and we lingered for almost two hours talking about art and culture. She asked how I'd become interested in skyscrapers and bridges and I told her the truth. It was an ego thing.

"An ego thing?" she repeated, laughing. Her cheeks were flushed pink. Maybe it was the wine.

"An ego thing," I retorted. "Don't act like you're surprised."

She asked me about my schooling, about my travels, about the most favorite thing I'd designed. I told her the truth about that too. There was no favorite thing. There were always regrets after the fact, when the pylons were sunk and the construction too far underway to make changes.

"You don't like your designs? Any of them?" she asked, as if this was the most tragic thing in the world.

"Don't you sometimes design things you don't like once you've executed them?"

"Yeah, but when that happens I melt them down and start over. I guess you can't do that with a bridge."

"No. They're a bit too permanent for that."

Everything about my life seemed permanent compared to Chere's. We never talked about her family or childhood. She had melted that down and reused it, and transformed into this fascinating woman with freckles and curls and ridiculously kissable lips. I leaned across the table and yanked her toward me, and kissed her long and hard. That was probably the wine too.

"Let's walk some more," I said.

An afternoon storm was blowing in. I told myself that was why I took her to the apartment on Rue de Cambrai—to get out of the weather. The doorman greeted me and took us upstairs in the ancient elevator. Jean-Marc had been the doorman here since I was a child.

"What is this place?" asked Chere, looking down the chandeliered hallway as I keyed in the code for the apartment.

"One of my childhood homes."

"Oh, wow," she breathed, as I struggled with the rustic knob and the decades-old wooden jamb. The door opened once I put my shoulder into it. As soon as it swung wide, I thought, *What are you doing, Price?* I tried to convince myself I only wanted to share the early nineteenth century architecture and decorative castings.

"You used to live here?" She followed me inside, mouth agape. It was a grand apartment.

"It's one of my parents' homes," I said. "They still live here part of the year. Not this part, thank God."

"Your parents are alive?"

I chuckled at her shock. "Does that surprise you? I'm not that old."

"It's just...you never talk about them. I assumed they weren't around anymore."

"They were never around." The words bled out, clipped and bitter. I walked through the foyer and into the main rooms, flicking on lights to illuminate high ceilings and finely carved shelves. The sofas and tables were slipcovered, and I didn't bother to uncover them. With the white, and the cold, bare surfaces, it felt like a mausoleum.

Chere followed me, taking everything in. "Why didn't we stay here instead of the hotel?" she asked.

"I hate this place." I softened my voice. "And the hotel's nicer. Room service, housekeeping, Wi-Fi. The modern luxuries." I led her to the window overlooking the street. We were six floors up, just as we were in New York. It never occurred to me until now.

"Are those your parents?" she asked, eyeing a portrait in the adjacent room. After glancing at me for permission, she walked through the double doors to get a closer look at it. The portrait was ten years old at least, snapped at some society function, based on my father's tuxedo and my mother's diamond necklace and earrings. Chere turned back to me with a grin.

"I never pictured you having parents. You know, being someone's son."

"I was their only son. I had everything a child could wish for," I said, and my breath slid through my lips in something that wasn't quite a laugh. "We came here every year, for holidays, for vacations. Once we spent an entire summer." I'd been a gawky adolescent then, not quite a teenager, but not a child. I stared around at the furniture, the walls, the grandness of everything which had barely changed over the years, then turned back to her. "I don't know why I brought you here. This house depresses me."

"Why?"

I crossed my arms over my chest and shook my head. "My poor little rich boy problems. Daddy never loved me. Mommy was always drunk. The nannies hated me for being a spoiled, self-centered brat. But I had all this." I waved my arm around the echoing, marble-floored chambers. My parents used to sit in one and shut me off in the other, with my nanny. The Turkish carpets were as bright as the sofas would be under their canvas covers, but when I was a child, everything seemed sad and colorless. I'd had no love and no power.

I didn't say any of this to her. I didn't know how to explain it, that early rejection that made me fear all rejection. If I didn't want love, then it wouldn't matter if I never got love. A captive in my dungeon was good enough. I used to dream of taking women captive. I dreamed of women who'd never want to leave.

I startled when she touched me. She put her arms around me and laid her head against my shoulder. "Really? Your mother was always drunk?"

"Yes."

"Mine was too."

I wove my fingers through her dark, glossy curls. "I can't say I had a bad childhood, not compared to yours."

"But you did. It's okay. You can be less than perfect around me. You can feel sad about things you didn't have."

"I had nothing before you."

My teeth clenched against more words, like I was giving a confession under torture. She blinked at me, her pretty face a mixture of confused emotions. Why had I brought her here? Why was I saying all this? Why couldn't I be normal and romantic, and just tell her how much I loved her? I started composing a poem in my mind. *You stood with me in the bleak, black house. Don't let the light fool you.*

Don't leave me. What if you leave?

"Is it still raining?" I moved away from her to look out the window. "Should we go back out?"

"Do you want to go back out?"

I could hear my heart beating in my ears. She stood very still with her hands clasped in front of her.

"Why don't you show me where you used to sleep?" she said. "Do you still have a room here?"

I shook my head, grimacing. "It's a guest room now. But you can see it if you like."

I showed her around the rest of the place, which was exactly what needed to happen so I could regain control of my shit. Not much had been done since I was here last. The place was protected as an estate of historical interest. They couldn't gut it and remodel. Even something as trivial as new faucet handles had to be approved. I explained all this to Chere as she stared up at the ceilings and walls. When we got to the guest room—my old room—she walked over to the window.

"I want to see your view. Did you look out here and daydream as a boy? Does everything look the same as it used to?"

I joined her, standing close to her and breathing in her scent. I put my arms around her and looked out the window where I had indeed daydreamed as a tormented boy. Back then, I would have done anything for attention and approval. Once, in a really dark hour, I'd sat on the sill and considered jumping to make my parents sorry. I imagined them mourning over my twisted, broken body, but I hadn't jumped, because I was too afraid of the pain.

"I was a horrible kid," I murmured against her ear. "I grew into a horrible adult."

"You're not horrible," she said, laughing softly. "Just a little rough around the edges." She turned to me and took my face between her hands. "You're wonderful. I love you."

And as I looked into her eyes, I realized everything I'd gone through was okay, because it had brought me here, to this moment, to her. I didn't trust my voice, or I would have told her how desperately I loved her. Instead I kissed her, turning away from my boyhood view. The kiss deepened to a grasping embrace and then an attack. *I love you, I love you, I love you.*

Don't leave me.

"Come here," I said. "Come with me."

I led her out to the center of the living room where my parents had held court with their rich friends and their rich endeavors, and tugged her down with me to the floor.

"What are you doing?" she asked as I slid a hand beneath her waistband.

"What does it look like I'm doing? I'm going to defile you on my parents' living room floor."

I popped her button and slid down her zipper. She stared up at me and lifted her hips so I could yank down her jeans. I held her gaze for a moment as I shoved fingers into her pussy and found her wet and ready.

"This floor is really…" She bit her lip. "It's really hard."

"I'm really hard, too."

I tried to cradle her as I shoved down my pants and positioned myself between her thighs. I could tell she wasn't comfortable, but when was she ever comfortable when we had sex? I groaned as I shoved inside her. Her warmth enveloped me and we were connected again. I was inside her and she was around me and Jesus Christ, I was so in love with her. This room was full of bad memories, but this would be a good one. I grasped her closer and wrapped my arms around her so I wouldn't bruise her as I fucked her across the floor.

"You're mine," I whispered. "I want you. I always want you."

"I want you too."

Her hips bucked up to meet my thrusts, and pretty soon the hard floor didn't matter, or the slipcovered furniture, or the fact that this was the room where my parents had always come to get away from me.

"Yes," she cried. "Yes, yes, yes."

"More?" I asked.

"*Yes.*"

I arched over her, driving in her hard, squeezing and pinching her, caressing her wherever I could reach. When she was close to orgasm, I grabbed her arms and yanked them over her head, and buried my face against her neck. I urged her on with dirty, filthy words until she came with a series of urgent gasps.

I held off a little longer, because it was so delicious to hold her writhing body here on the floor of this awful place. It was weirdly necessary to take her here in this room, in this house with so much sadness. Maybe that was why I'd brought her here. I didn't know, and by the time I started climbing toward orgasm, I didn't care. I gazed down at her and thought about the poem I'd mentally composed earlier. I'd have to write it down for her. *You trembled under me as I fucked you in that bleak, black house...*

When we finished, I helped her up and into the bathroom to put herself back to rights. It wasn't even dinner time yet. "There's more I want to show you," I said. "Let's get out of this tomb."

* * * * *

I took her from the stark stillness of my parents' *pied-a-terre* to the touristy squalor of the 18th Arrondissement. We skirted around the Moulin Rouge even though I thought Chere might enjoy it. Too many people, too campy, and honestly, Chere was a hundred times sexier than the topless burlesque dancers inside.

Instead we walked the gritty streets and browsed the North African marketplace. I was blond and white enough to raise some eyebrows, but Chere fit in with her bronze skin and old New Orleans features. When I was a teenager, I came here to get away from my parents' glittering world. I learned to scowl and be tough, and posture, and throw attitude. I wanted so badly to belong here, where life seemed real, where money changed hands in small, sweaty, wrinkled bills, where my parents would never dare go. *Stay out of the Goutte d'Or*, my mother would scold, but I knew *Goutte d'Or* meant *Drop of Gold*, and even before I used the name for my first bridge, I thought that was the most beautiful name for anything ever. I felt like a man in the Goutte d'Or, even if the ageless women behind the stalls would smile at me like I was a boy.

They smiled at me now just as they had then, with curiosity and a quiet patience. We walked from the Maghreb areas into the Chinese district and then to a row of Indian shops with windows full of gold and silk.

"There's so much to see," said Chere, gripping my hand as we moved through the crowds. "My eyes..."

She wasn't complaining. She was delighted. People crowded around us, working class men and women ready to celebrate the weekend. We ducked into a small, pungent cafe with a view of the Sacré Coeur, and shared a table with an elderly Indian couple who spoke over us in rat-a-tat Tamil. I looked around in sudden realization, watching time turn in on itself. I used to come to this cafe. I was sure of it. It was a different place then, with different decor and different food on the menu, but the view was the same.

Chere caught my gaze and put a hand over mine. "Don't you like the food?"

"I like the food. I'm not that hungry." I fed her banana and rice from my plate, and thought that I probably shouldn't have fucked her on my parents' living room floor. I suffered this sociopathic desire to possess her, to use her, to mark her as mine. The Indian woman at our table looked between us with a knowing smile.

"You're not from here," she said in French. "You and your lady." She gestured toward Chere.

People were so bold in the 18th Arrondissement. "We're not from here," I admitted. "I'm showing her around. I used to stay nearby when I was young."

Chere didn't understand a word of our conversation, for all her French name and her Creole heritage. She gave the woman a crooked smile and the woman gazed back with a curve to her thin lips. She had dozens of rings on her fingers, stacked all the way to her knuckles in a jumble of silver and gold. Chere stared at them, entranced.

"She'd love to see your rings," I told the woman, and she offered her hands for Chere's perusal. While Chere bent over the bands and gemstones, I studied the woman's bindi, the bright third eye within the wrinkles of her brow.

"You seek clarity," she murmured under the raucous noise of the cafe.

"What?"

"*Clarté,*" she repeated in French. "You're drawn to my bindi because you have many questions. You seek a balance of your higher and lower selves."

"I'm perfectly in balance," I lied. "I'm drawn to your bindi because I've visited India and Asia many times."

"You travel so much?" She nodded. "Of course. You seek. You search. But all answers come here."

She reached out, but she didn't touch me. Instead she touched Chere's brow, letting her fingertip linger atop some invisible bindi. *Higher and lower selves.* My low self was all over Chere all the time. We had no balance, as this complete stranger had so bluntly pointed out.

"Tell her that her rings are beautiful," said Chere.

"Tell her I said *merci,*" the Indian woman replied with a smile. "You both have questions, *non?* Many questions. But at least you are together."

I didn't know whether to take that as a compliment or an insult. Her companion demanded her attention and they left soon after, allowing a group of teenagers to crowd closer to our table. Chere asked about my conversation with the woman. Instead, I told her about bindis and my travels to New Delhi and Mumbai.

We left the cafe shortly afterward and walked aimlessly toward the red light district, taking in life in all its raw and ugly glory. We slipped into a half-empty club and drank licorice-tasting cocktails as a pair of dark eyed women belly danced onstage. Their fingers jangled noisy hand cymbals, and golden tassels flew as they tossed their hips.

Chere watched like she was drinking it in and didn't want to miss a drop. I did nothing to distract her, only held her hand as the alcohol seeped into my veins and the flashing clang of the cymbals resonated through my brain. *I love you,* I thought. *I love being here with you. I love watching you take it all in.*

I've been here before, but it feels less wistful when you're with me.

"Gold is beautiful. I should use more gold," she said. "It's so vital. Silver is cool and elegant, but gold is..."

She lost words and started gesturing to the gold painted walls and ceilings, and the gold-edged veils swishing from the dancers' hips. I could see the lights from the stage reflected in her eyes like miniature stars.

"What do you like better?" she asked me. "Gold or silver?"

I shrugged. "I like them both. I like them in combination. They change one another when they're together."

I understood about gold. Some of my buildings had gold trim or burnished bronze fittings, but all my bridges were silver or light metal. Silver was for streamlined strength. Gold was for crazy, gaudy shit.

"I wonder if I could do that," she said, turning back to the stage. "Belly dance like those women?"

"I'm sure you could. Maybe I'll order you to do it for my pleasure," I said, sliding a hand up her thigh. "I've seen your hips move like that when I fuck you. I've seen them jerk like that when you're under duress."

I gave her a look, and she shivered and pressed closer to me. I took her chin hard and kissed her, tasting licorice and sweetness. I wanted to make her hips move. I wanted to make her gasp and struggle for air. I wanted to give her something to remember this by.

When the belly dancers finished their set of frenetic shimmying, and our small cordial glasses were drained, I pulled her up and out into the street. It was getting late now, and I hurried, making pathways for her amidst the burgeoning tourist crowds. I found a shop we'd passed earlier, its windows full of gold necklaces and chain link chokers, earrings and baubles. It was cheap stuff, metal shit. While she tried on some bracelets, I spoke in French to the man behind the counter.

"Do you have gold?" I asked. This was the Goutte d'Or, after all. "I need a gold and crimson ring."

He studied me and gave a nod. All these vendors had merchandise they didn't put out where anyone could see it. He produced a gaudy, ruby-encrusted ring from behind the counter, but I shook my head.

"No. Delicate. For her."

I nodded over my shoulder to Chere, who was trying on beaded chokers and peering at herself in a mirror.

"Ah," he said. "*Attendez.* Wait, if you please." He spoke to his partner and disappeared behind a beaded curtain into the back.

"Look," said Chere, returning to my side. She wore a sleek, ebony bead choker that came closer to her aesthetic than anything else in the shop. "It's like a collar," she whispered. "Isn't it?"

I shook my head. "It's not strong enough. It'd break into pieces the first time I squeezed your neck."

I thought of the summer we'd met, of our date at the Empire Hotel. I'd basically raped her that evening, and snapped a pearl necklace off her neck. Broke it, destroyed it. Pearls had flown everywhere. I wondered if she was thinking about that too.

She left me to try on a few more chokers, but none of them was half as lovely as her solid, honest, plain, brown collar. They were jewelry. Her collar was the real deal, a symbol of submission that bound her to me. *You're mine. I own you.*

"*Monsieur?*" The man returned from the back, holding a small gold circle pinched between his fingers. "How about this? Delicate. Crimson and gold."

He put it in my palm, and I felt lingering warmth, like he'd just taken it off a mandrel. It wasn't what I'd imagined in my mind's eye—it was better, more *vital*, as Chere had said. I'd pictured a small red ruby in a gold band. This ring had striated garnets, two of them in a line that was both jagged and pleasing to the eye. The band was thin and lightly hammered. Delicate, but vital. We haggled briefly over price, and then Chere drifted back to me.

"Give me your hand," I said.

She blinked and let me slide the gold and garnet ring onto her finger. I realized too late that it was her left hand, the hand for engagement rings and wedding rings. It was merely the hand closest to me. "It's a collar for your finger," I said, so she wouldn't misunderstand. "And a memory of tonight."

I watched her study the ring. I felt self-conscious because I wanted her to like it. I loved it. It seemed perfect to me, but she was a jewelry designer and maybe she wouldn't feel the same. Maybe I should have just written her another poem. Words were ephemeral, mere air. Rings were...

Fuck. Did she like it?

"It's too loose," she said, looking up at last. Her eyes were shining. "If it's a collar, it needs to be snug."

And I realized her eyes were shining because she was about to cry, and it suddenly seemed like this ring was my heart laid bare in front of her, and *did she like it?*

She smiled at me through those gathering tears, and then I knew she loved it as much as I did. The jeweler looked at the ring on her hand, gauged the diameter with a practiced eye, then took it in the back and returned with a perfectly sized band, as if he'd measured her finger. Nice and snug.

"It's so beautiful," she said, staring down at it.

"You can wear it on either hand. Whatever you like. But I want you to wear it all the time, even when you can't wear..."

The shopkeeper was standing there, and very likely understood English. I touched her neck and she knew what I meant. I paid for the ring, and the restless angst that had risen in me at my parents' house was calmed again. She was mine, all the time. Her collar was back at the hotel, and now she had this ring she wouldn't be allowed to take off.

It was clarity. The ring was gold and bindis, and my high self and my low self, and all the deep, emotional things in between.

CHAPTER SEVEN: COMMITMENT

As soon as we returned from Paris, Price got busy. I tried not to take it personally. He'd missed a lot during his week away, so if he had to work late, and was gruff and distracted when he returned home, I had to accept it like I accepted all the other bad things he did to me.

But I also thought, *you gave me a ring.*

What does this ring mean?

I chose to believe it meant some kind of commitment, even if our relationship was an infuriating dance of advance and retreat. I hadn't imagined the look in his eyes when he slid it on my finger. I hadn't imagined the new closeness that developed in Paris, even if he was in full retreat by the time we returned. He could insist on rules. He could hide behind protocols and training, but I knew that the other man was there, the Price who was full of love and tenderness and poetry. Those thoughts sustained me through every stringent session in the dungeon that week.

Outside the dungeon, away from my Master's unforgiving bondage and forms of torture, life went on. Vinod emailed that he would be visiting New York, and invited me to design some pieces for upcoming fashion lines. He sent me megabytes of photographs and sketches, and his excitement was contagious. I began to work exclusively on men's accessories, solid, classic tie bars, rings, cuff links, and I found it a welcome change from the whimsy of women's pieces. Men's fashion was so much more straightforward, and I spent as much time in my studio as Price would allow.

As for my dear friend Andrew, it was nearly two weeks before I could make plans to see him. He wasn't amused. He glared at me as I walked across the Big Apple Diner, making sure I comprehended his displeasure before he swept me into a hug.

"It's been too long, girl," he said, pressing his blond curls to my cheek.

"I know."

He drew back and looked at me hard. "No, I mean, it's really been too long. I know I come after your work now, and your fucked-up life with that sociopath you call Master—"

"Shut up, please. I have a million things to tell you." I shoved him down into the booth and sat across from him, picking up my menu. As I scanned the familiar offerings, I wiggled my ring finger at him. "Notice anything new?"

He grabbed my hand and yanked it toward him, gazing down at the strikingly delicate, gold and garnet ring. "Wow, babes. It's pretty. He gave it to you?"

"In Paris," I said, nodding. "After a crazy day. He took me to his parents' house—"

"You met his parents?" Andrew's eyes went wide. "Are they sociopaths too?"

"They weren't there, and he's not a sociopath. He took me all over Paris, to all these out of the way streets and shops and this little cafe overlooking the Sacré Coeur. You would have loved it. There was so much to see, so much to paint. So much inspiration."

The waitress came and took our order, and then I gave Andrew a quick and dirty recap of the trip, from my ill-advised viewing of *Heart-Lust*, to my meeting with Vinod Sushil, to our trip to the Goutte d'Or.

"So...but..." Andrew looked flustered and grabbed my hand again. "What does this *signify*?"

"It's a collar for my finger. I'm supposed to wear it all the time."

"Or you get punished?" He rolled his eyes.

"You know about our thing," I told him. "You're in a power exchange relationship too."

"Yeah, but mine isn't so smothering."

"You don't have rules and consequences?"

He lowered his voice and leaned closer to me. "Not like you. I hate that I can't see you whenever I like. This whole once-a-week rule is creepy."

"He wants me to focus on work right now."

"Bullshit. He wants you all to himself." The waitress delivered our food, and Andrew bit into his sandwich with barely restrained vitriol, before violently dunking a French fry in ketchup. "I mean, even this," he said, waving a hand around. "Making us meet in a public place? How many hours did we hang out together at your apartment when we were in school? I mean, what the fuck does he think is gonna happen? I'm super flaming gay."

He announced that very loudly. An older gentleman at a nearby table turned to Andrew with a speculative smile, but Andrew was taken, and he wasn't in the mood to flirt. I watched him murder another French fry.

"It's not a big deal," I said. "We like this place. Does it really matter where we hang out? Why are you getting so upset?"

"Why *aren't* you getting upset?" he shot back. "I mean, your thing with Price isn't normal or healthy. All this controlling structure, all these rules?"

"There aren't that many rules."

But there were. I wasn't supposed to meet with a man, any man, gay or straight, unless it was in a public place. I had to show Price any texts I exchanged with men, including Andrew and Vinod. There were rules about what I wore and where I went, and where I slept, and when I could orgasm. There were rules about speech and posture and how I reacted to punishment, and now there was a rule about wearing a gold and garnet ring.

"If you don't see how freaky it is—" Andrew said.

"We like freaky, remember?"

He glanced over my shoulder. "Shit. Speaking of freaky, Professor Predator has entered the building. Keep your head down. Maybe he won't notice us."

It was easy for me to blend in, with my plain brown hair and short stature, but Andrew stuck out like a beacon with his huge mop of blond hair. Within moments, Martin Cantor, ex-professor, rejected lover, was standing beside our table with his takeout order under his arm.

"Hi, kids," he said.

I looked up at him in exasperation. We were in a public place, yes. I wasn't breaking any rules by talking to him, but I'd still have to tell Price that I'd run into Cantor—and based on his mood the past couple weeks, he would likely react in a fucked up way.

"How are you, Professor Cantor?" said Andrew.

"I'm good. How are you? How's the painting?"

"It's great. I've got a website now, and lots of studio contacts. I've been busy."

"Glad to hear it." He turned to me next, his eyes dark and probing as ever beneath his scruffy salt-and-pepper hair. "And Chere Rouzier, what a pleasure. I haven't seen you since graduation. How's the real world treating you?"

He'd seen me at graduation on Price's arm, and his skewering regard told me everything I needed to know about his feelings on that.

"The real world's been treating me well," I said. "I've set up a studio, and I'm designing for a pretty big client. I can't say anything about that yet."

"So big you can't drop names, yeah?"

"I guess."

Cantor always made me feel defensive. We never would have worked out. "I just got back from Paris," I said, to change the subject. "It was beautiful."

"Ah. Price dragged you there for the architectural conference?"

"Well, I didn't go to the conference. But I soaked up a lot of inspiration." *And got punished. And got a new ring that means...something.* "It was an eventful trip for me," I finished lamely. "I was happy to go."

"I guess it helps to have rich, powerful friends."

Cantor had always been a squirm-inducing combination of nice and nasty. Now I was the one murdering French fries as he stood there with a judgey expression. "So, you and Price are still together?" he asked, trying to sound casual. "All is well?"

"Everything's great."

"I'm glad to hear it."

Andrew watched the two of us, a bemused smile at the corners of his lips. He was the one who'd coined the term "Professor Predator" based on Cantor's inappropriate interest in me. I guess Cantor had been a pretty good metals professor, but now that I'd graduated, all we really shared was an awkward past.

"Well, okay then," he said, shifting his takeout bag to his other hand. "I'm back to Norton. You two take care."

As soon as the door shut behind him, Andrew burst into laughter. When I frowned at him, he laughed louder and leaned his forehead down to the table, like he was bowed under the weight of all the fuckupedness.

"It's not funny," I said. "Not that funny, anyway."

Especially for me, because I'd have to tell Price about our random run-in. I didn't tell Andrew that, because I didn't want him to start going off again about Price's possessiveness and his crazy rules. I knew. I lived by them. My ass died by them. It wasn't funny at all.

"He still wants you," Andrew said when he caught his breath.

"He's an old horn dog professor. Whatever."

"He's the same age as your horn dog Master, and you don't think he's old."

"You're barely legal, so what do you know?" I said, flicking a finger at him. "And you're with an older guy too."

"Craig is your age, honey, so don't call him old."

"How is Craig?" I asked, to move the conversation along from Cantor. Andrew indulged me by launching into a recitation of their divine life together, with all Craig's wonderful qualities, and all the things they'd done in bed the night before. I was glad they were so happy. I was happy too. I was.

I had a ring, and poetry. Yes, there were a lot of rules, but for now, for Price, that was the way things had to be.

To play it safe, I texted Price that I'd talked to Cantor before I even left the diner. I figured that way he could get over his initial irritation and maybe forget about it altogether before I saw him again.

He texted back right away. *What did you talk about?*

Nothing. We just said hello. He asked what I've been doing. He talked to Andrew too.

How is Andrew?

I breathed a sigh of relief. *He's fine.*

Then, a moment later, he texted, *Did you feel anything for him?*

I knew he didn't mean Andrew. Did I feel something for Cantor? Hell no. *He actually made me uncomfortable*, I texted. *He asked about you. About us.*

What did you say?

That everything was great. I didn't feel anything for him, I swear. I never did.

That was mostly true. The only reason I'd considered getting into a relationship with Cantor was the crushing loneliness I'd felt while Price was away. I thought a moment and added, *I only love you.*

Too risky to say that. Too effusive. Price got freaked out about love, even though he claimed to love me. There was no reply for a while. Then: *Be a good girl. Busy afternoon. I'll see you tonight.*

* * * * *

We had Chinese takeout for dinner. Price asked them to throw in two extra pairs of chopsticks, and then set them aside until we went to the dungeon. Now the chopsticks were rubberbanded onto my breasts, with a nipple pinched between each set.

He'd warned me I wouldn't always like belonging to him. He'd warned me there would be days I'd hate the dungeon. I hated it right now. My nipples burned and my shoulders ached from the rope harness holding my bent arms behind my back. My ass clenched on a huge glass plug that had only made it into my ass with copious amounts of ginger-infused lube. My knees hurt from the hard floor as I tried to focus on my Master. His hand twisted more tightly in my hair.

"Keep your mouth open," he demanded. "When you're on your knees, your mouth is open and your attention is on my cock."

I knew that. He'd taught me that, but sometimes I forgot, and sometimes I just freaking had to take a moment to swallow. My eyes streamed with tears, not from the chopsticks or the ass plug or the sharp, hair-pulling scolding, but from the sheer physical trauma of having his cock shoved into my throat again and again. I sucked in air through my open mouth, and breathed through my nose when he plunged forward.

I couldn't remember anymore how it felt to give a relaxed, sensual blowjob. With Price, they always involved violence, and a terrifying lack of control. I opened my mouth as wide as I could, teetering on my knees, trying to seem hungry. No one ever said being a sex slave was easy. I desperately wanted a washcloth to wipe my face.

"Get up," he said, yanking me by the hair.

I wouldn't say he was being any rougher tonight than he normally was, but there was some added tension in his gaze, and his grip. Because I'd spoken to Cantor? Maybe he thought I was lying when I said I didn't feel anything for the man. Maybe when I told him I loved him, he thought I was overcompensating out of guilt. Again, the angst between us came down to a simple lack of trust.

But I couldn't talk things out with him in the dungeon. I wasn't allowed to talk, and he was naked and hard and not in the mood for talking either. He walked me over to the spanking bench and battened me down, hooking my collar to the structure and binding down my waist and legs. My arms were still cinched behind my back in a lattice of rope knots, and no amount of squirming could free them. When I was finally restrained to his satisfaction, he went to the chest of drawers and returned with a heavy strap.

So it wasn't going to be a long, drawn out session tonight, just a beat down that was probably going to make me bawl. The strap brought real tears, not just the moisture forced out of my eyes through choking and physical exertion. He didn't reserve the excruciating blows to my ass either, but worked over my thighs until I strained against the bench.

"Is your mouth open?" he asked as I cried and panted. "Open your fucking mouth in case I want to put my cock in it. You're mine to use, in whatever fucking hole I want." To illustrate that fact, he whapped the strap across the base of the butt plug, then walked around the bench and jammed his cock between my parted lips. I wanted to tell him that I felt hurt and exhausted, and that my asshole felt fucking abused by that plug, and that I hated the strap he clutched in his fist.

"If you can use that mouth to talk to Cantor," he said, fucking my face, "then you can sure as hell keep it open to serve me. And if you can't, we'll get out the cock gag and do a little more training."

Oh, shit, the cock gag. A thick, hard, intrusive piece of rubber that was as humiliating as it was uncomfortable to wear. I opened my mouth wider and let him pound me out. *Please, no cock gag. Please, I'm sorry I spoke to Cantor. I'm sorry he ever almost came between us. In the end, I chose you...*

"Keep your mouth open," he said, pulling away from me. I did, even though a thick string of drool dripped from my lips. He gave me a dozen more blows with the strap, until my butt throbbed with a hot, deep pain, then he put the strap away and returned with a vibrator wand. I eyed it in dread. *Please, no, please, not the forced orgasms.*

He shoved it under me, positioning the wand between the bench and my body, and setting the oscillator squarely against my clit. Did it feel good? Yes. Was I wet and riled up from everything he'd done to me so far? Yes, but I knew this horny, trembling pleasure was about to be turned against me in the very worst way.

He walked behind me, grabbed my shaking hips, and impaled me on his cock. My nipples throbbed in their chopstick prisons as his shaft pushed inside, rubbing along the unforgiving glass plug in my anal channel. His cock felt awful and wonderful at once, slipping, sliding, hurting me, filling me, taking up every inch of space inside me at his whim. He slapped my ass as I keened from the pleasure and pain. The wand vibrated my clit, building to an intensely sharp orgasm. I contracted on the hard intrusions inside me, my whole body shaking from the power of the release.

I clenched my teeth to stop myself from babbling *Oh God, oh God, oh God.* He slapped my sore thigh. "What did I tell you? Keep your damn mouth open."

I obeyed. I opened wide and made frantic, crying sounds through my lips. He loved to show me that he could take over my body and command me to do almost anything. At the moment, I was nothing at all, except *his.*

The orgasm started to wane and my body quailed with exhausted satisfaction, but the wand continued on, stimulating my clit. I tried to arch away from it, but the strap around my waist held me captive to the continuing vibration. He continued to fuck me, steady, hard thrusts that felt even fuller now that I'd come. I knew it would go on like this for fifteen or twenty minutes, that he would purposely hold off his own orgasm as long as possible to make me suffer the maximum amount of overstimulation.

I tried to relax. I tried to let another orgasm come even though I didn't want it. I came again, and a few minutes later, again. My clit felt swollen and overused, but the vibrator did its work, and physiologically, my body kept coming in a continuous volcanic eruption.

Mentally, I thought I was going to die.

I can't, I can't, I can't. My mind kept telling my body that it couldn't go on any more, that my ass was spasming and my pussy was all used up, and my nipples needed freedom, and my clit couldn't bear one more moment of stimulation, but the man tormenting me didn't care. The fucking went on, and the vibrating went on, and the orgasms came, each more painful than the last.

I was very close to breaking the rules and begging. I was so close. The only thing that kept my open lips silent was the threat of the cock gag on top of everything else. Instead I whined plaintively in my throat, my voice rising and falling with the rise and fall of each forced climax. I sounded like an animal. I felt like an animal, reduced to the ungoverned physical operation of my body. I tried to arch my pelvis to get my clit some relief, but it was only momentary, and then the sensation was there again.

Oh, please, oh, please...

At last I felt his thrusts quicken, felt his organ pump ejaculate inside me. At last, *oh God, thank you.* He stepped back, his cock slipping out of me after stuffing me to the hilt. He walked around and undid the chopstick clamps, and twisted my nipples between his fingertips as sensation came roaring back. I waited—mouth open—for him to switch off the vibrator, but he didn't. He stared at me, and I stared back at him as I was required to.

Shit, oh shit. I can't. You asshole. I hate you. I love you. How can you do this to me?

He was making a point. He owned me. He used me however he liked. He reduced me to an animal when he felt like it, and let me be human again only on his schedule. I got it. He made me squirm and jerk through three more painful, unwanted orgasms before he finally switched off the satanic wand.

"You can close your mouth now," he said as he undid my bindings. "But never forget who that mouth belongs to."

I gave him a baleful look. It wasn't the slavey kind of look he probably wanted. Once he untied my arms, he steered me over to the cage, and I thought, well, I probably deserve this for looking at my Master that way. I crawled inside and curled in a ball.

My clit was swollen and sensitive, and my ass was still impaled by the massive butt plug. I curled my arms over my sore breasts and lay on my side, wishing the cage had a pillow or a padded cushion or something. Price was always mean to me in this dungeon, but today he'd been really mean and I was having trouble accepting my lot. Slave, thing, toy, holes to fuck. His to abuse. He was a sadist. *He'd warned me.*

Tears trickled down my cheeks as he moved about in the harsh light, putting the dungeon back to rights. I hated the way he lit everything, all my pain and humiliations showcased to a ridiculous degree. I wanted to hide in the darkness. I heard his footsteps when he returned to the cage, sensed him standing right beside it, but I didn't turn to him the way I was supposed to.

"Look at me," he said in a sharp voice. "Don't act like a fucking brat, Chere, or we'll start over with orgasm number one."

I sighed and turned to look up at him through the bars.

"I wasn't hard on you today because you talked to Cantor," he said. "I was hard on you to remind you that you're mine."

Duh. We both knew that. I didn't know why he still felt threatened by Cantor. Nothing had happened between us. *You're the only one I've ever wanted. Why won't you believe that?*

"Martin Cantor is a player," he said. "He wouldn't have known what to do with you. He couldn't have made you happy."

And you do? I thought, shifting on my sore ass. Frustration bubbled over inside me, so I broke my speech restriction and blurted out, "Why are you so jealous?"

He kicked the cage, an immediate, sharp reprisal that made me jump. I huddled back against the bars but there was no more kicking, just a trip to his chests of torture implements. He returned with the terrible, huge, plastic cock gag in his hands.

I shook my head, for all the good it did me. He opened the door and reached in, and dragged me to him by the O-ring on my collar. I shut my lips against the thick shaft and earned a slap on the cheek for it. I opened and swallowed as he forced the gag in. It distended my jaw and compressed my tongue, and made me feel very, very sorry that I'd poked him when he was already in a bad mood.

"No talking in the dungeon," he said as he secured the gag's straps behind my head. "You know the rules. Fucking follow them."

I glared at his chin. *Yes, I know the rules. I also know you're fucking jealous and possessive and you don't trust me any farther than you can throw me, and it's starting to make me fucking sick.* I submitted to everything he required of me, even this choking, humiliating cock gag. He might give me a little trust in return.

He shut the door of the cage and I seethed in there, ass plugged, mouth plugged, his slave in disgrace. My hands were free. I could have reached behind my head and undone the gag. Nothing was stopping me but his possession and his will. He stood and watched me, hands on his hips, my unchallenged owner. My evil tormentor. He would always win, no matter the fight, no matter the consequence.

He held my gaze, wanting me to surrender, but sometimes I just couldn't do it. Sometimes I felt so angry and frustrated within our dynamic that I wanted to explode. A shiver rocked me, and then I did explode, beating the bars with my fists. I wanted to bust them open, or at least bend them a little to show that he couldn't control me completely. But I couldn't do anything, because his cage was too strong, just as he was too strong.

When I finished my pointless tantrum, he knelt beside the cage and glared in at me. "Do it again," he said in a terrifyingly calm voice, "and I'll beat your ass until you can't walk." He reached between the bars and grabbed my hair, giving it a firm yank. "Behave, you fucking brat, or we'll train in here all night."

I ground my teeth against the rubber cock in my mouth and considered that threat. No, no more tonight. I knew my limits. I lay still in the damn cage and tried to relax my body until he was satisfied that I was under control. Then he opened the door and dragged me out, and positioned me on all fours beside the bars I'd chosen.

Because I'd chosen this prison.

I thought about that as he fucked me again, triple penetrated me with the gag in my mouth, the plug in my ass, and the cock driving inside me, gentler now, but still steady and firm and as endless as he could make it. I braced my arms on the floor and cried tears he couldn't see as he pinched and twisted my sore nipples. When I arched my back up against him, begging without words for him to stop hurting me, he pinched my nipples harder. Drool and muffled sobs leached from behind my gag until he came inside my cringing body. I had chosen this. Even now, I had no desire to leave. Even now, all I wanted was to satisfy him.

Later, when I was clean and human again, he led me to the guest room, to the place I slept when I was in disgrace. I was allowed to talk now, but I chose not to. I had nothing to say that wouldn't anger him or muddy the waters between us. Instead, I reminded myself silently, over and over, *you chose this. You chose this. You chose this.*

When I was settled under the covers, he sat on the edge of the bed, gazing down at me with a probing expression. Even without words, without tears, he knew I was struggling. He knew that when I didn't talk, I was the most upset of all.

"If you don't like the things I do to you," he said, "you can leave."

I shook my head. "I'm never leaving you. Never."

Some tautness in his body slackened. He took my chin between his fingers and kissed me, one of those fervent kisses that was more like gnawing on my mouth, and I surrendered to it with my own quiet violence. He kissed me like he was protecting me, like Cantor might still spring up at any moment and doom our relationship. For an intelligent man, Price could be pretty stupid, but then, I'd never been much of a genius in the relationship department myself.

His kiss gradually gentled, but I remained a roiling mess of confused emotions. After he left, I took an hour or more to fall asleep. He exasperated me and thrilled me and wrung me out until I was clinging to the last shreds of my sanity. Jesus, I loved him, but I wasn't completely sure that I should.

CHAPTER EIGHT:
A PLACE OF PEACE

Chere was quiet on the drive to work the next morning. She sat beside me in the back seat of our chauffeured sedan, dressed in a dark shirt and a long, patterned skirt. She wore skirts all the time now. Easy access, and she didn't seem to mind it. I could take her right now if I wanted, either with my fingers or my cock, or my mouth. When she was surly and sub-hungover, I wanted to eat her alive. Out of respect for the driver, I restricted myself to holding her hand.

"What's on the schedule today?" I asked in the stultifying silence.

She turned her head a little and brushed her curls back from her face. "Just work. I have some new designs that Vinod approved. He's coming in a couple weeks to see the samples, and I want to have everything ready to show him."

"Busy, busy," I said. "What about other clients?"

She gave me a look. Vinod Sushil Enterprises was taking up the majority of her time, and I was taking the rest of it.

I shrugged. "You should always be looking for new clients. If you get too busy, you hire people to work under you. I have fourteen associates at Eriksen."

Her bottom lip pushed out in a pout. "I want to do it myself. I don't want other people to do it for me."

"I do things myself. The other people assist me."

She turned to look out the window. I clasped her hand more tightly, not allowing her to pull away.

"You tell me that..." She paused and drew in a breath. "You tell me that I belong to you. You won't let me see other people or talk to other people without losing your shit, and yet you push me toward world domination."

She was being sassy and she knew it, which was why she wouldn't look at me. I'd allow this little rebellion, to a point. More cage rattling. It pleased me at least as much as it unhinged me.

"First of all, I don't 'lose my shit,'" I said. "I protect what's mine, which is what you signed up for. And I'm not 'pushing you toward world domination,' I'm explaining that business grows or contracts. There's no coasting, Chere. Onwards and upwards."

"Can I get my feet under me first? Vinod's a huge client with a lot of lines, a lot of opportunities. I'm sure more business will come."

I snorted. "Not from him. He's going to put your work out under his own name and keep you a secret as long as he can."

"But in the contract—"

"In the contract, his name is bigger than yours. It's all right." I let go of her hand and stroked the concerned lines on her face. "That's how you start. But Vinod Sushil isn't the height of your career arc. He's the starting point. Don't forget that, no matter how busy he keeps you, no matter how much smoke he blows up your ass."

Her half pout turned into a whole pout and a sigh as she curled her hands together in her lap. She still wore the ring I'd given her on her left hand, where an engagement ring would go.

"Chere," I said, touching her knee.

"What?"

Ugh. It was hard being her lover *and* her owner *and* her career mentor. It was hard being everything to her, but I couldn't let any of it go. Without control, fears crept in. Fears for me, fears for her. Fears for us.

"Don't bitch out," I said. "I'm only trying to help."

After a moment of tension, she turned toward me and rested her head against my shoulder. Her hand crept back into mine and I held it, stroking my thumb across her palm. "I love you," I said. I didn't say it very often, because I didn't know what it meant, and I didn't want to diffuse the word's power by saying it all the time, but at moments like this, when she returned to me, when she *surrendered*, it was all I could think to say.

"I love you too," she said.

With my other hand, I dug in my briefcase and pulled out a folded sheet of paper. I hadn't been sure I'd be able to give it to her. I'd written it in a haze of guilt over my jealousy of Cantor, jealousy she'd called me on in no uncertain terms. The fact that she'd been in a cage at the time didn't soften the blow.

Why are you so jealous?

I don't know, starshine. Maybe because I love you so fucking much.

"This is for you," I said, forcing myself to hand it over. Her face lit up the way it always did when I gave her poetry, but seriously, it had been easier to give her other people's poetry. Writing my own feelings felt like opening up a vein on the page.

"You don't have to read it now," I said.

"May I read it now?"

"If you want."

She let go of my hand and opened the paper, and looked down at the words I'd written early this morning, while she was asleep.

He strokes her, presses her palms, her arms,
Her lips, her body, her cool skin.
She wants to be hurt and held. He wants her to huddle
Inside his walls and sleep.

"He" was me, of course, and "she" was Chere, and the poem was part of what I felt last night, but not enough. They never expressed enough. My poems were clumsy sketches, not paintings, and I never managed to rhyme like the old school poets. There was no rhyme to us, no reasonable organization.

"I didn't get to huddle with you last night," she said when she finished. "I missed you."

"I missed you too," I said, although that wasn't what I meant by that line. I meant that I wanted her inside me forever, where no one else could get to her, or influence her, or lure her away. When I wrote *sleep*, I meant *surrender*, but she'd already done so much surrendering last night that I couldn't bear to put that on the page.

"Thank you for writing this," she said. "It's beautiful. I love when you write things for me." She scooted closer and rested her head on my shoulder as she had before. As she scanned the poem again, she asked, "What are you working on now?"

"What?"

"At work. You always ask what I'm working on, but we never talk about your work. What are you working on at Eriksen Architectural Design these days?"

"Everything, all the time." At her small grimace, I added, "Right now, we're concentrating on some skyscraper designs for Jakarta. There's an engineering aspect to it because of the expense, and the earthquake systems that have to be in place. Not to mention the corruption in the local contracting companies."

"Will you have to go to Indonesia?"

"Eventually. Not yet. I have people to do it for me, people who work for me," I said, referencing our earlier conversation.

She looked down at the poem. The driver stopped hard at a light, shifting us in our seats. A horn blared behind us.

"Do you still want me?" she asked, turning her face up to mine.

"I always want you."

"You know what I mean." Her jaw went tight. "Are you tired of me yet? Tired of dealing with me in your house? In your life?"

I gave her an arch look and tapped the paper she held in her hand. "Didn't you read the poem, starshine?"

"Sometimes I think you only write them for me because you feel guilty. You always give them to me after I've been punished for something."

It was my turn to look away from her, out the window. "That's because I'm impressed by your strength," I said. *And afraid of it. I live in terror of the day you discover you don't need me after all.* "To answer your question, I'm not tired of you yet." I turned back to her. "Do you think it's easy to write those things? I do it so you won't leave. If I wanted you out of my house, I'd stop writing poems for you. Once that happens, I'd give it about a week."

She did what I hoped she would do, which was laugh and smile at me, and touch my hand. After that she folded up the poem and put it into her work bag with all her other notes and journals and plans. She thought

I was joking, but I wasn't. What did I really give her, besides a lot of pain and control? She wouldn't take my money and I couldn't offer any romantic ideal of love. What did I provide to make her love me?

Poetry. A ride to work every day. A collar for her neck and her finger, and hopefully enough earth-shattering orgasms to make her stick around.

* * * * *

Time flew by, hours at work, hours in the dungeon, meetings and projects and a couple more trips for Price's work. Fall turned to winter, and Price and I celebrated our first naked Christmas and New Year's together. I wish I could say things had grown more comfortable between us by that point, but they hadn't, not really.

A lot of the tension came from my work, the challenge of trying to remain a surrendered submissive while I built an ever-expanding brand. When Vinod Sushil mentioned my aesthetic in an article for Modern Art and Design, things blew up to an alarming degree. A hundred people contacted me within a week: design houses wanting to hire me, agents wanting to represent me, rich, famous people wanting me to design exclusively for them.

It was hard to believe sometimes that a few years ago I was a sex worker with no motivation and no future. How things had changed from the Miss Kitty years. Of course, the more popular I got, the more I worried that one of my old johns would recognize me and show up at my studio to harass me. I felt afraid when I remembered my old life. I worried about who would crawl out of my past and try to destroy me by denouncing me as a fake and a criminal. I worried about losing everything if and when my old career was revealed.

I didn't share any of this with Price. The work alone had already brought so much stress to our dynamic, and talking about my past always made things even tenser between us. Instead, I pushed it out of my mind and concentrated on work and inspiration, and tried not to freak out at all the demands for a "Starshine Original." This success was everything I'd worked for, right? Andrew was thrilled for me, and Price...

Well, Price was supportive. He was happy for me, but he never let me forget that our dynamic came first, and in a way, that kept me on an even keel. It was hard to get an inflated ego when you spent almost every night on your knees having some type of torture inflicted upon your body. It was hard to get a big head when your sexual orifices were no longer your own, and when you were often forced to sleep in a chastity belt so you couldn't soothe your aching pussy.

The more my schedule blew up, the more his control tightened, and I tolerated it as best I could. Most days I felt happy, even in the dungeon. Even in the chastity belt. The harder he held me, the better I felt about myself and about my life, because he was worth every sacrifice. His smiles, his poetry, the way he touched me after he hurt me, like there was no one else besides me in the world. I felt surrounded and protected in a very powerful love, whatever he chose to call it. Slavery, ownership, our "dynamic." It was all the same thing: my love for this complicated and deeply protective man.

I was existing in this calm and surrendered bliss, working in my studio on a cold day in early January, when an unexpected visitor came to my door. The visitor pushed it open slowly, which meant it wasn't Price, because he always threw the door wide and strode in to greet me with an owner's confidence. No, the door opened by increments, like this visitor wasn't sure he'd be welcome to enter.

When he finally came in, I wished he hadn't entered.

Simon Baldwin, tall and dark and frighteningly familiar, stared at me from across my studio.

I stared back, alarm bells going off in my brain. It wasn't only that we had a traumatic past together, and that our most recent interaction had involved a trip to jail for Price. No, it was that I wasn't allowed to have *anything to do with him*, and he was standing here in my studio, and oh, shit, Price's head would fucking explode.

"Hi, Chere," he said. "Nice studio."

"What...what are you doing here? How did you get in the building?"

He shrugged. "My accountant's office is on the eighth floor. So you're in the jewelry business now, huh? How've you been?"

I blinked at him. He looked the same, perhaps a little heavier since he'd stopped the drugs. All I could think was that Price might show up anytime, and all hell would break loose.

"You have to go," I blurted out, not even taking the time to return his greeting. "You have to leave right now."

"Why?"

I was having a panic response. My breath literally felt tight in my chest. What had Price done to me, that I was so afraid to speak to men? But it wasn't just any man. It was *this man*, the one who'd brought so much devastation to my life.

"You just... You have to go, Simon. I'm not supposed to talk to you."

"Well, that sucks, because I was hoping to talk to you." He sat in the chair by my desk, making himself comfortable.

"I'm not supposed to..." I began, but then I stopped, because I was a grown woman and it was weird that I wasn't allowed to talk to people. With a brutal flash of lucidity, I realized that I was just as controlled by Price as I'd been controlled by Simon and his addictions. *You use me for sex the same way Simon used me for money*, I had screamed at Price once. *To get your fix.*

I thought I was finished questioning the validity of Price's love for me, but within three minutes of seeing Simon and experiencing the feelings he evoked in me, I felt riddled with doubt.

"No," I said, putting my head in my hands. I didn't even know who I was talking to. "No, I can't deal with this right now."

"I know you're busy," Simon said. "I've been following your success in the design mags. Vinod Sushil, huh? Not bad."

"Yeah, I've been really busy. That's why I can't talk to you. I'm sorry."

"Chere—"

"You have to leave."

"Look, I know I hurt you," he said, speaking over me. "I know I've been an asshole to you hundreds of times. Thousands. But give me a chance to say what I need to say. I've changed, I promise. Every day is a battle to stay clean, but I'm trying."

So he was still sober. There was that, at least, that he'd turned into a better person. Some quiet desperation in his features made me sit back in my chair and push Price's glowering expression out of my mind for the moment.

"What do you want to talk about?" I asked. "I don't have a lot of time. Please, make it quick."

"Can we start by talking about you?" He looked around my studio with a dazzled expression. "I mean, wow, Chere. It's like you've reinvented yourself. You must be really proud. Are you proud?"

"Yes," I said through my teeth. "I'm really proud."

My curt tone registered, but the essence of Simon hadn't really changed. Fucked up or sober, he was still incredibly self-centered. Despite the fact that I clearly wanted him to state his business and get out, he lounged back in the chair, crossing one leg over the other.

"I'm reinventing myself too," he said. "Everything in my life is better. The art's going well. Everyone said I wouldn't be able to create good work now that I'm sober, but it's just a different process. It still works. Everything's good, but there are some issues I need to work through. Stresses."

I glared at him. *Sorry about your stresses, asshole. I also have stresses. Get to the point.*

"So, part of getting sober is taking real and concrete steps to change your life. There are these twelve steps that are part of my rehab program. Step four is to take a 'searching and fearless moral inventory' of yourself, and I've been doing that, you know? As you progress through the program and take this inventory, one of the things you do is go back to the people in your life that you've hurt and talk with them, and try to make amends."

I put my hands over my eyes. "Simon, I can't."

"Please, just hear me out. I need your help with this."

When I looked up, he had his fingers steepled in front of him, pressed together like he was praying.

"The thing is," he said, "I'm really haunted by a lot of things. I'm haunted by you, and I don't want to be. I'd like to spend time with you now that I'm sober, so we have better memories. I'd like to talk to you, and apologize, and show you that I'm not that person I was when I was with you."

I shook my head. "I can't. I just... I want to help you, but it's not possible."

"Why not?"

"Because I'm in a relationship with someone else now. A really intense relationship."

"I don't want to get back together with you or anything. I won't make unwanted advances. I just want to talk through what happened in our relationship, and try to come to a place of peace."

"I don't want to do that," I cried. "It took me a long time to get over you. Years of sadness and loneliness and wondering what the hell was wrong with me, that things went so bad. I'm in a different place now and I don't want to revisit what we went through. I want to forget it. I want to forget you!"

"But I need your help! Every day—" His voice rose and broke off. He rubbed his forehead, this man who was so different from the strung out Simon I used to know. "Every day is a struggle," he said in a quiet, tortured voice. "I'm trying to become a better person. Every day, I'm trying to get better."

"Why do you need me for that?" I could feel myself softening toward him, even when I didn't want to. Drugs had been his life. I couldn't imagine how hard it had been to get off them, and stay off them this long.

"Really...the change has to come from yourself," I said. "I don't see what I can offer you."

"No one knows me like you. I loved you. We were together for *ten years.*"

But we weren't together for ten years. We were together maybe a third of that time before everything went haywire. I could still remember the sickening slide, watching him lose his shit little by little, day by day, until he was a completely different person. I wasn't there for him then. I'd done nothing to stop him from disintegrating.

And now...if I did nothing to help him...what if he slid into that hell again?

"What exactly do you want from me?" I asked.

"I would like us to be friends." He knotted his fingers together. I could see the ever-present paint flecks under his nails. "Can you come over for dinner sometimes?"

"No, I can't."

"Can we meet somewhere for lunch then?"

I sighed, shaking my head. "I'm in a relationship with someone. He wouldn't like it."

"It would just be friendly. A time to talk. Or I can come here. I think a friendship between us would keep me honest. It would remind me..." He paused and bit his lip. "It would remind me how easily I can hurt someone. How deeply I'll hurt everyone if I fuck up and fall back into the drugs again."

He was honestly, truly desperate. I could see that. I was beginning to feel a little desperate myself. "I can't be your sober coach. I don't know anything about drugs or rehab or sobriety. I can't be responsible for helping you stay sober."

"You don't have to be. I'm responsible for staying sober," he said forcefully, "just as I was responsible for my actions, and for the way my actions hurt you. Now I'm responsible for making things right. You were such a huge part of my life. I don't want to hurt you by taking you back to those times, but I don't know if I can get better without your support and forgiveness. I know that sounds selfish. I just want..." He unlaced his fingers and threw out his hands. "God, I want to move on."

"I want to move on too." That was the damn truth. I wanted all of this to be over, our past disappeared, but as Simon said, it wasn't that easy. We'd been through things. We'd pretty much been through hell.

The rough part was that I could never explain this to Price in a way that would be okay with him. Even sitting here and talking to Simon this long...he would murder me for it, and probably stick me in the cage for hours afterward. He wouldn't understand, perhaps could never be made to understand.

But did that mean I couldn't help this man who'd been such a part of my life, who was here begging for a path to peace?

"Fuck," I said. "This is really difficult."

"I know. It took me forever to find the courage to come see you. But God, I'm taking all of this so seriously, Chere. I can't go back there again. I can't."

"Can I have some time to think about it? Some time to talk to my partner?"

"Yeah, sure," he said, even as I thought to myself that there was no way in hell I could talk to my partner. There was no way in hell Price would allow me to help Simon in any way, shape, or form.

No, I was asking for time so I could summon up my courage, and figure out if it was possible to elude Price's control enough to give Simon the help and closure he needed. Was Simon's sobriety worth it?

More to the point, could I stand by and let Simon ruin his life a second time? When I still carried such guilt that I'd let it happen the first time? Price said it wasn't my fault, but I couldn't make peace with that opinion. Maybe this was my chance to find some peace too, even if I felt like my head was about to explode.

"Can I come back tomorrow?" he pressed. "Will that be enough time for you to think about it?"

"No. Don't come back here."

"Then how can I contact you?" He frowned. "Jesus, you're acting kind of crazy. This guy you're with, is it the same dude who attacked me at that gallery?"

"Yes."

"What's the deal with that?" He looked at me far too steadily, with too much knowledge of my weaknesses. "Chere, have you gotten yourself into another bad situation with your hotheaded star-chitect friend?"

He had a lot of balls to ask that, considering he'd been my first and most monumental bad situation. Price was nothing like him. Was he?

"He's not my *friend*," I said. "We're together. He gave me a ring and everything."

Simon stared at it when I showed him. "You're engaged?" He sounded shocked.

"Not officially engaged," I admitted. "But we're pretty serious, and brutal honesty here, he hates your guts. He's not going to want me to see you. He doesn't want me to have anything to do with you."

"If he doesn't like it, tell him to fuck off."

I pondered telling Price to fuck off, especially as it related to Simon. The idea was too ludicrous for words.

"I want to help you get over our past together," I said. "I can understand how it haunts you, but I'm not going to damage my current relationship in the process. Just give me some time to figure things out."

His skeptical regard unsettled me. "I guess we all have problems. Maybe we can help each other. Do you need help with this guy?"

"No," I snapped. "Do you still have the same number? Don't call me. I'll call you, okay?"

"When?"

I sighed. "When I can. Do you want to be friends or not? Friends are patient with each other."

But Simon Baldwin had never been patient, or a very good friend, even before drugs took over his life. I finally got him out of my studio by telling him I had a deadline to meet. I breathed a sigh of relief that Price hadn't come by for a morning blowjob. Most days, he waited until the afternoon.

God, I had to calm down. I needed to figure out how to help Simon attain mental peace without wrecking my own hard-fought sanity. I wasn't sure there was a way to do it, which really sucked. Maybe I could just tell Price that I needed to help Simon find closure. Maybe he would understand if I explained it deftly enough.

No. Fuck. He'd never understand, and he'd never allow me to see Simon again. I was supposed to have zero contact with my ex. Zero. Never. Nothing.

I was definitely fucked.

CHAPTER NINE:
SO FUCKING SORRY

I watched the whole thing happen in real time, watched it on a window on my laptop as a meeting continued around me. There was no audio on the surveillance feed, but I saw the intensity and duration of their conversation in high-definition detail. It seemed like they spoke forever, and there was real emotion, real connection in the way they conversed. She hadn't seen Simon in months, not to my knowledge.

Not to my knowledge.

But had she? He was sober now, and rich as ever. He was good-looking, if you liked hipster vampire types. Hell, she'd gone to see his fucking painting in Paris, fucking *cried* over that shit. It seemed as though the question wasn't "Does she still have feelings for him?" but rather "How intense are the feelings she still has?"

Shit. Shit. Shit.

No Simon, nothing to do with him, ever. That was our agreement. Hell, that was one of the first rules I'd established with her, and she had no "out" clauses to fall back on, no reasons why it might sometimes be okay to see him or speak with him. It was never okay.

I didn't leave the meeting to go down and interrupt them. I was tempted to barge in there and throw him through the frosted glass door, but no. I didn't do it, partly because I wanted to catch them in the act if she was fucking around on me, and partly because I was paralyzed by fear.

Instead, I watched until he left, clinging to every shake of her head, every expression of distress. Was it distress, or longing? Why the hell would he come here and have an emotional conversation with her after all these months?

I had to know. I waited to be paged by the receptionist. I waited for Chere to come to me and admit she'd met with Simon, and confess everything they'd talked about, but she didn't, and it slowly became clear to me that she wasn't going to. She bent back over her work, with no signs of guilt about the crime she'd just perpetrated before my eyes.

Of course, she didn't know she was on camera, any more than she'd known when I spied on her with my hunting binoculars from across the street. I'd never admitted that I'd had cameras installed before she occupied her office, so I could watch her intermittently throughout the day, like during tedious planning meetings. I had every right to do it if I owned her. The cameras were one more layer of protection, one more layer of control.

Whether she knew about the cameras or not, she had a responsibility to come tell me what had transpired. Our rules regarding her and other men were very involved and very specific, and she'd broken about five of them between nine-thirty and ten o'clock.

I thought, okay, maybe she's afraid to admit what happened. Maybe she's trying to think of the right words to say. Maybe she's working on a deadline. Maybe...

Maybe what?

I took her out to lunch. Nothing. Nothing but distant thoughts and nervousness, disguised in overly cheerful conversation that made me want to slap her. *Admit it. Admit what you did, you faithless bitch.* After lunch, I took her back to her studio and sat in the chair he'd sat in, and ordered her to blow me. Still nothing. No confession. No mention that he'd been there, sitting exactly where I was sitting.

Now I stared at her across the dinner table, giving her the benefit of the doubt. Meeting with Simon was a huge fuck up. Maybe she was still gathering the courage to come clean. But maybe...

Love lies.

Maybe she had no intention of telling me. If that was true, it was the beginning of our end. If she was choosing Simon—*Simon*—over what we had together, then I was done. I was done trying to save her, I was done trying to make her life better and more fulfilling. I was done twisting myself in knots trying to make us work. I was done risking my heart, bleeding poetry onto paper. If she wanted Simon...

But I'd let her speak first. I'd make her speak, if she didn't elect to confess on her own. We went into the kitchen to clean up after dinner. I offered her ice cream. She asked for wine instead, and I thought, now. Now the confession will come. She just needed a little alcoholic fortitude to admit what she'd done. We took the wine into the living room and sat on the couch together. I waited.

Nothing, damn it. She was wondering when I'd take her to the dungeon. I kept her naked at home, always ready. She wanted to play.

I was tired of fucking waiting. I put my glass down on the side table and asked, in as casual a voice as I could muster, "Did anyone visit your studio today?"

There was an awful, soul-destroying moment when she thought about lying to me. I could see it in her features, in her expression. *Oh shit, he knows. I better lie. Could I get away with a lie? No, I couldn't.*

At least she realized that. Her expression turned from panicked to wary to grim.

"Yes," she said. She put her glass down and crossed her arms over her breasts. "Simon came to see me. I didn't invite him. He just showed up."

"And you told him to leave?" I asked, making her uncross her arms. No hiding. I wanted her naked as shit right now.

She watched me a moment before she answered. "Yes, of course I did. That was the first thing I said to him, that he had to go."

"And did he go?"

"Yes."

I stared at her. She glanced away, and then back.

"He did go, eventually," she said in a tight voice.

"What did you talk about?" I was very proud of how level and calm I sounded. I didn't feel that way inside.

"We didn't talk about anything."

"He was there a long time to be talking about nothing."

"How do you know that?" She went from defensive to belligerent. Typical old-school Chere tactic. It wasn't going to save her now.

"Tell me what you talked about," I prompted, tugging her collar's ring to focus her. "I'm angry enough that you met with him. Tell me what I want to know."

She slid back on the couch, away from me. "No, you tell me how you know all this. Were you spying on me? Jesus fuck, do you watch me? Is there a camera in my studio?"

"Of course there is. You think I don't like to look at you throughout the day?"

She was heading full speed into outrage. "You seriously installed a secret camera in my studio? You didn't think that was something I might want to know?"

"It's something you should have assumed, considering our past together. The cameras aren't the issue here."

"The *cameras*?" she said, getting to her feet. "Plural? How many cameras are there?"

"Sit down. Sit the fuck down or the ass beating will commence immediately. We need to talk."

"Yes, we need to talk." She sounded snarky, but she obeyed me and sat her ass back on the couch. "I can't believe you've been spying on me all this time. What am I, your personal zoo animal? A fish in your fishtank?"

"Yes, you're a very beautiful fish I can watch whenever I like."

"Where are they? Where are the cameras?" She sat up straighter and looked around the living room. "Do you have them here in the house? In the guest room?" She paled. "In the dungeon? Have you been taping all the shit you do to me?"

"*The shit I do to you?*" I repeated with a warning note in my voice. "Is that what it is? Shit? You agreed to be mine, Chere. We have a relationship, a dynamic that is all encompassing, to include"—I marked off each word on my fingers—"surveillance, obedience, control, exposure, and whatever the fuck else I want. You live here in my house, by my rules. What's the rule about Simon?"

"That I can't see him," she said. "But I had no control over what happened. He came to see me!"

"You didn't work that hard to throw him out."

"Because he was upset. He was stressed out."

"About what?"

She rubbed her forehead. "About his sobriety. About these steps he's working through, and our past, and trying to find some kind of peace between us."

I let out a breath. The emotion, then, made sense.

"I mean, I couldn't just throw him out," she said. "He was begging for my help. I kept telling him I couldn't help him, but he seemed so desperate."

I frowned at her. "That's exactly the shit he pulled on you before, acting pathetic and desperate so you would 'help' him. I forbade you to see him for a reason. He's a user, Chere."

"He's sober now."

"That's not the kind of user I meant. He's a *user*," I said, with frustrated emphasis. "He'll use you for the rest of your life if you let him. Did he ask about you at all? How you're doing? How your work is going?"

"Yes! He said he was proud of me. And he asked if I needed help when I told him about this, about you. About how you wouldn't let me interact with him, even as friends."

"As friends. Perfect." I gave a nasty laugh. "Because he has so many qualities you want in a friend."

"I almost let him die once!"

Jesus Christ. Tears. She was crying over him again. I couldn't take it.

"I almost let him die last time because I didn't engage with him," she said. "Am I supposed to do that again?"

"Yes." My voice sounded too loud, too harsh. "Yes, you're supposed to have nothing to do with him. Why is that so hard to understand? We've been over this, Chere. We've fucking been over it."

I thought of Paris, of the brutal punishment I'd given her for merely going to look at one of his paintings. This was so much worse. She wanted to *help him*. She still *cared about him*. She was *crying for him*...again.

"If you don't stop crying, I swear to God I'll fuck you up. I'm not even kidding."

She swiped tears off her cheeks, but she only cried harder and made more. So many tears. Some of them were probably for me, for fear of me, and worry about what I was going to do to her. She'd been a very bad girl, not just to see him, but to hide it from me. To feel so much for him, to allow him this pity and concern...

"Maybe instead of punishing you, I should just punch you in the face so you can remember what it felt like. Then you can decide how much you want to help him."

She buried her head in her hands and bawled. Jesus, the fucking drama. It was so hard for her to admit when she'd been bad, when she'd done something wrong.

"I'm not going to punch you." I touched her leg, trying to calm her. "I'm going to make this easy for you, okay? Listen to me. You're not helping him. It's not your job to save him from his past mistakes. You're not seeing him again."

"But he needs help. He seemed really upset, really conflicted."

"He deserves to be conflicted for the things he did to you." I narrowed my eyes. "It's like you want to see him again. Like you want to become involved with him again. I don't fucking understand."

"I'm trying to exorcise my demons too," she said. "I had a life before you, a very complicated one. I have feelings that don't involve you. I know that's hard for you to accept. Since I moved in here, my entire life, my emotions, my feelings, my friends, all of it has become this tiny little box that only has room for you."

"You chose that. I warned you. You said you wanted that!"

"Simon is still sick, Price. He's still struggling to stay sober. He needs me."

"I need you," I said, stubbornly clinging to my own guilt, my own past mistakes. "I need to protect you from being hurt by him again. I watched it happen once, and it sucked like hell. I'm not going through that again. No. You belong to me now. I get to decide. I get to protect you."

The more I argued, the more she fought back. I liked her fighting spirit sometimes, but when she was fighting for her abusive ex-boyfriend, it fucking pissed me off.

"You're smothering me," she yelled. "You don't want to protect me. You're jealous of Simon just like you're jealous of every other fucking man in the world because you're such a fucking insecure wreck. You don't trust me to be around any other human with a penis. Why? Jesus. It makes me hate you sometimes."

I flicked a glance over her naked body. We hadn't played hard in a while. There were no marks on her. Maybe I needed to leave a few marks to get her straightened out. "I think you better watch the way you talk to me," I said. "You're going to be punished for hiding your meeting with Simon. Don't make me punish you for your manners too."

"Fuck my manners. Fuck your rules and protocols and protective bullshit. You don't love me, you don't care about me. You haven't changed at all. You still have no fucking heart underneath all your grasping, possessive, posturing bullsh—"

I stood before she could finish her sentence, and yanked her off the couch.

"Walk," I said, turning her toward my bedroom. Toward the dungeon.

She started to resist, then thought better of it. Surely she understood she'd earned a punishment. If she'd decided to make it worse with more screeching and disrespect, that was her choice. Her misstep. Her own fucking mistake she'd have to live with.

"Please, don't," she said, trying to pull away from me. "Let me calm down first. I can't. Please... Please, I'm so sorry."

Nothing she said loosened my grip or slowed our inexorable progress toward the dungeon. I loved Chere. I loved her too much to let her lose her shit like this. I loved her too much to let her go backward, even if forward motion was about to cause her a whole lot of pain.

CHAPTER TEN: SURRENDER

Oh, shit, I'd fucked up. The look in his eyes...

Shit, I was so scared. I resisted even though I knew I'd earned this. We had a dynamic to follow, a system of rules and expectations, and I'd broken every one of them. I felt awful and out of control, but still, I didn't want this.

"Stop," he said, halfway toward the bondage rack. "Stop fighting me. You're going to get what you deserve. No more, no less."

That's what I was afraid of. Most of the time I loved coming to the dungeon with him. I loved the way he treated me like a sexual science experiment, a bundle of female nerves on which to practice pleasure and pain.

But I knew there wasn't going to be any pleasure this evening. He got out the manacles, the ones I'd fashioned to his specifications, back when I had no clients and no prospects. He put them on my wrists in a quick, businesslike way, and hooked them to the chain and pulley system in the ceiling. At the push of a button, the chain moved upwards, and soon I was straining with my arms to the sky, barely able to dance around on my toes.

I felt horribly vulnerable in this position. It was hard to balance on the balls of my feet, and with my arms up out of the way, my entire body was exposed. *At least you're not straddling the "bad girl" horse*, I thought. But I still felt pitiful and scared.

A set of nipple clamps came next, and shit, a clamp on my clitoris that bit hard into my sensitive flesh. The clamps were the heavy, painful kind that tightened when you moved, and I made whining sounds just to process the pain.

"Hush," he said, slapping my ass. It wasn't a playful slap. It was a hard, stinging slap that made me jump, which made the clamps tug, which made me cry out again. He shook his head and went for the gag I hated most in the world.

No, I almost said. *No, no, no.* But I wasn't allowed to talk in here, and he was angry enough. He forced my mouth open with his fingers when I started to sob, and shoved the hard rubber cock gag into my mouth. Fuck. I fucking hated being gagged and bound like this, and the punishment hadn't even started. He buckled the gag behind my head as my clit and nipples throbbed. Sometimes wearing clamps made me feel like a sexual, erotic creature, but sometimes it just felt shitty and painful, and *owww*, I never wanted anything to touch my clit again.

He stood back and looked at me, and I made the saddest eyes I could. I felt sad. I felt fucking awful. I felt naked and endangered, while he was stern and perfect, still dressed in his designer sweater and pants. He took off his belt and doubled it over, and I braced for the first blow.

When I felt the stinging impact, I screamed behind the gag. This was punishment. It wasn't supposed to feel good and it wasn't supposed to be easy to take, so there was no warm up, just a hard, wicked strike across the ass. I pulled on the chain and bounced on my toes, and waited in dread for another blow. *Ow, ow, ow. Ah, God.* By the fifth blow, I was in tears. On the sixth, I tried to twist away, even though it was against the rules. He righted me and turned my face back to the wall.

"Don't you fucking try to escape," he said. "We're just getting started."

By the time he put aside the belt, I was a trembling, drooling, snotting mess of apology, but the paddle came next, an oval shaped instrument of torture that burned like a brand. Every time he smacked my ass, an almost unbearable sting would be followed by a deep ache. My nipples hurt, and each jump and jerk reminded me of the clamp on my clit. It was impossible not to squirm away when the pain was so hard and so sustained, but he only braced a hand at my waist and forced me to stand still while he paddled my ass with the other hand.

His closeness comforted me in some way, but it also made me more frantic, because now I was struggling against him and he was still hurting me, almost more than I could bear.

Through my cries and my drool, the cock gag remained fixed between my lips. In between blows, when he let me rest and suck air through my nose, I worried at the gag with my tongue, but I couldn't push it out. I couldn't take it out on my own. Only he could do that, and it involved so much loss of control that I was frantic with it.

At last he stopped, holding me while I heaved in my efforts to survive all the pain. The clamps came off, and then the manacles came off, so I could stretch my arms and rub the ache out of my shoulders. The gag stayed on, even though I begged with my eyes to be released.

But he wasn't finished yet. I was hauled over to the bad girl horse, with the blunted triangular top. He made me straddle it and ordered me to keep my feet on the floor, even though that made the unforgiving ridge dig into my already hurting clit and pussy.

"Hands up," he ordered, as I tried to push myself up off the horse and give my pussy some relief. "Lace your fingers behind your head and leave them there."

He left and returned with a whip, the short, black, evil one he favored when he wanted to deliver pain on top of pain. He whipped my ass, my flanks, my back, my breasts, each stroke raising a pink, burning welt that felt too sharp to deal with. There was no rest in between, no time for me to concentrate on how much my pussy smarted as I jerked and jumped on the horse. A few times, my hands came down to shield my body. I was sorry afterward because he whipped me harder, until I put them back where they belonged.

Through all of this, he made me look at him. Every few blows, he'd stop and gaze into my eyes, and I understood why. I knew by now why he insisted on that rule. He was taking me as far as he could without breaking me. In some way it made me feel cherished, that he was being careful and closely monitoring me as he carried out this torture. In another way it made me feel like I was slowly going insane, that I was even allowing this to happen. Why didn't I jump off the horse? Why didn't I run?

I only wanted to help Simon. Why are you hurting me so bad?

But the hurt went on. He was hurting me for yelling at him, and hurting me for lying. *I'm sorry, I'm sorry.*

There was no sex, not even a blowjob. I prayed for a blowjob. I would have given him the world's most ardent and salacious blowjob if he would only stop, but no. I'd been punished before, but never this long and this hard, with no sex and no respite. My body heaved with sobs, not that I thought they might move him. I simply couldn't hold them in. There was snot everywhere.

When I started to choke on the gag, he took it off and wiped my mouth, and made me lie face down on top of the padded bondage table. He cuffed my wrists, waist, and ankles so I couldn't move. I gritted my teeth together so I wouldn't start pleading *please, no, no, no more.* My whole body felt bruised and bloodied, even though I knew there wasn't any blood. He was an expert at keeping hurt on the surface.

He flogged me with a heavy leather flogger all over my back, until everything hurt the maximum amount possible. Ass, shoulders, calves, thighs, back, everything burning, and then he turned me over and bound me again, and made everything on my front hurt. Breasts, hips, stomach, thighs. He made me spread my legs and brought the flogger down on my pussy in a fiery punishment that made me arch in agony.

I wept for mercy. I couldn't talk, but I wept, and finally, when my pussy felt like one big center of throbbing pain, he put the flogger and everything else away, and let me rest.

I lay just as I was, arms bound over my head, waist bound, legs bound apart with my pussy on display. For all I knew, he might begin again. If he did, I'd have to accept it. That was our deal. I belonged to him, to cherish or to hurt, to nurture or destroy.

At the moment, I felt destroyed.

When he returned from putting everything away, he checked over me, touching all the places he'd hurt me. I knew he enjoyed examining the welts and bruises. He released me and made me stand while he inspected my back. Then, finally, after he'd touched and caressed all the marks, he pushed me to my knees to assuage the hunger my pain and suffering had created in him.

He was rock hard, straining at the front of his pants. When he undid his fly, his cock flopped out and whacked me in the face. It was something we might have laughed at in other circumstances. Now, I clutched at him and opened my mouth, and sucked him with frantic concentration, my eyes fixed on his face to make sure I was pleasing him.

Because when someone had just punished you that severely, you pretty much wanted to do whatever they demanded. As he pushed into my throat, yanking my hair, banging my tonsils over and over, I felt myself relax. My body still hurt, but my punishment was over, and I could take this violent blowjob if that's what he wanted. I was his, absolutely, one hundred percent his to use, which I supposed was the outcome he'd hoped for after beating me for almost an hour.

He came in my throat with a growl, jamming himself into me as I choked and tried to swallow. As soon as he released me, I coughed and collapsed on the floor. I hurt everywhere. I didn't want to move.

"Look at me," he said, pulling me back to my knees.

I stared at him, biting my lip. *Please, no more punishment. Please, I feel like I'm about to die, and if you're still angry with me...*

"Who owns you?" he asked.

"You do," I rasped through my sore throat. "You own me, Sir."

"Who makes the rules in our relationship?"

"You, Sir."

"I do, and I punish you when you break them. I punish you when you treat me with disrespect. You don't get to sleep in my bed tonight. That's a privilege for good slaves who obey and show respect."

I pressed my face against his hand, but there was nothing to say. He wasn't asking a question. He wasn't asking my opinion. He was telling me I had to sleep alone tonight, in the guest room, the horrible room that made me feel conflicted and isolated. It pretty much meant the punishment was going to continue all night.

A few tears squeezed from my eyes, but when he led me out of the dungeon, I went to the guest room as I'd been told. He didn't bother with a chastity belt. There was zero chance of me touching my clit after everything it had been through, and I was too depressed to feel sexy anyway. Orgasm denial was only fun when you wanted to orgasm. I would rather have died.

I took a shower even though the water pressure hurt my welted skin, because I needed to wash this day off me. After that, I crawled into bed, eager to find refuge in sleep. I still didn't know what to do about Simon. I didn't know if Price would forgive me. I'd reset our already negligible levels of trust back to zero. Fuck, fuck, fuck.

Price and I had plenty of happy moments, but at times like these, when everything looked bleak and frightening, I would start to think, *I can't do this anymore.* I liked the good, sexy pain we shared most nights, but the punishment pain slaughtered me. Not the marks on my body. Not the manacles and clamps and drool and snot and shame. I mean, those were bad, but what really killed me was the loneliness, the rejection, the feeling of failure, when all I ever wanted in life was to succeed at something and be proud of myself.

Men all over Asia would soon be wearing my accessories. I was creating a gold and diamond set for an A-list actress to wear to the Oscars. And yet here I was, curled in a ball of self-hatred and doubt. I wanted Price to love me. I wanted the questioning and jealousy to go away. I wanted us to fix each other, but some days it felt like we were only making each other more broken.

I'll never be enough for him. Why do I even try?

I started to sob, and it wasn't the sobbing from earlier, triggered by sustained and agonizing torture. No, these tears were from emotional pain. Oh God, it hurt. Everything fucking hurt, and I felt so fucking alone.

* * * * *

Shit. Fuck. Fuck.

Fuck.

I lay in my bed and watched her on my tablet, because yes, there were cameras everywhere. Yes, I loved her that much, and yes, I'd beaten the shit out of her in the dungeon. I had to. Our relationship had rules. We had a fucking dynamic to follow. I was the Master and she was my slave, and she wasn't allowed to be around hurtful people or get herself into hurtful situations.

Even if I felt like maybe I was the most hurtful person in her life right now.

She was crying, really crying. Unlike the smaller cameras in her studio, the guest room camera had audio, and I could hear the misery wailing out of her throat, even though she tried to muffle it in her pillow.

I put my hands over my ears. I could still hear. Sometimes I loved the sound of her crying. Sometimes I licked her tears off her face like they were expensive wine. Sometimes her tears got me hard and made me want to fuck her to oblivion, until she cried another kind of tears, from sheer exhausted pleasure.

Sometimes, like now, her tears made me feel like throwing myself out a window.

I got up and started to pace. I couldn't go to her. Tonight was about teaching her to appreciate the connection we had by taking it away from her. Our connection, our relationship, our *dynamic*. My beautiful, sad Chere wore my collar even now, while she lost her shit in a fetal position.

Fuuuck.

I buried my face in my hands and then stalked back to the tablet. I could mute it. I could close out the camera feed and go to bed. Even then, I knew I'd hear her, like a dog could hear its owner's car from two blocks away. Instead, I went and stood outside the door. Maybe I could just stand here. Maybe that would be enough. I thought I'd just stand here until she stopped sobbing, but while I was making those plans, I'd already turned the knob and stepped inside.

She was so naked, so sad and pitiful. I thought, *she understands our dynamic. She knows that when we aren't together, we're lost.*

I knelt on the bed and pulled her into my arms. She turned into me the same way she'd curled into her pillow, and erupted in more tears.

"Please don't leave me," she said, clinging to my neck. "I'm sorry."

"Hush." I just wanted her to stop crying. I thought I would die if she didn't stop crying, me, the sadist who reveled in tears. "You need to settle down," I said.

"I can't live if you don't love me," she whispered against my neck. "I know that's weak. I know it's stupid."

"Shut up." I held her against me and rubbed her back, and traced the welts on her ass. "I love you, which you already fucking know. But Chere..." I brushed the tears from her trembling cheeks. "I can only endure one kind of love. I can only have all of you. I can't share you with anyone else, do you fucking understand that? Especially not him."

"I wouldn't. I wasn't..."

I put a finger over her lips. I didn't want another argument, not now.

"I'm sorry," she said instead. "I'm trying. I want to give you all of me." Her voice sounded strained. "But not all of me is...perfect."

Fuck, I thought to myself. *Fuck, fuck, fuck.* I was the most imperfect person in the universe, and somehow I had this slave who wanted to be perfect for me, and I fucking wanted to fling myself from a window because I obviously wasn't enough for her.

"You're fine," I said. "You fucked up, you were punished, it's time to move on. You need to calm down now. You need to sleep."

"Please don't leave me," she said again.

"Don't fucking tell me what to do."

"I'm not telling. I'm pleading."

I sighed. "I'll stay here until you calm down."

But I stayed longer than that. I stayed until she finally fell asleep in a twitching, shuddering heap of exhaustion. Even after that, I stayed to watch her sleep, and tried to convince myself that it was okay to love her even if I hurt her. Did all my love for her cancel out the control, the sadism, the pain? Her apartment across the street haunted me. Someone else was renting it now, but should she have been there instead? Would she be happier there? Should I have stuck to my binoculars and let her find her own way?

What if she'd ended up with Cantor? Or back with Simon, or some other asshole who didn't take care of her? At least I cared. I told myself that in the silence, repeated it like a mantra as a nighttime of minutes ticked by.

Then it was breakfast, and Vera was there, and Chere was dressed for work so none of her marks or bruises showed. In some way, the housekeeper was a chaperone, preventing things from getting any worse between us. I hoped things would get better. I slid a paper across the table.

You're so beautiful, I'd written. It was shorthand for a longer phrase, a poem, a piece of our past. *Look at what you do for me*, I'd told her once, as she regarded her wrecked reflection in the mirror. *You're so beautiful.* Now it stood for all the sacrifices she made in our relationship, and my acknowledgement of them. She gave a soft sigh and placed it beside her plate. I imagined her collar around her neck, and then my hand instead, choking her, stealing her breath. Stealing everything from her. But I would always, always try to give things back.

Her phone buzzed on the table next to her.

She looked down at the message, then at me. She handed it across the table before I even reached out my hand. There was no name at the top of the screen, just a number. Another message came before I could read the first one.

I know you said not to call, but it's been almost a day now.

Chere, please. I'm searching for peace.

I let out my breath in a huff. "He's searching for peace," I said. "Asshole."

A moment went by before she spoke. "I guess sobriety's hard, especially when you have demons."

"He's a fucking demon." I pushed a few buttons and blocked his number, then put the phone down beside me. "I'm going to keep this for a while."

I could tell she wanted to argue, but the memory of last night was still brutally present between us. She bit her lip and looked down at her plate. "For how long?"

"Until I'm sure he's moved on." *And until I'm sure you've moved on, you and your kind, codependent heart.* Did I really think she wanted to get back together with Simon? No. I might worry about it every once in a while, but I knew it wasn't realistic.

Did I think he might fuck her up again, while fighting his demons? Yes, I absolutely did. I think he wanted nothing more on earth than to get in some parting shots now that Chere was happy and successful without him.

"What if someone else tries to call me?" she asked.

"I'll give you your messages."

"I think Simon needs me."

"Like he needed you before?" I frowned at her. "Like he needed you when he sucked the life out of you and used you for his own fucking weakness? No, Chere. Not again. I'm taking this phone for your own protection, and I'm warning you..." I waited until she met my gaze, because this warning was serious as shit. "Do not dare let him draw you in again. No contact. Zero contact. Do you understand?"

This was why I'd punished her so harshly last night. To get her to the point where she would look up at me and say, in complete and utter surrender, "Yes, Sir. I understand."

"Promise me," I said.

"I promise."

And that was more than surrender. That was her word.

CHAPTER ELEVEN:
A PLACE TO HIDE

I kept Chere's phone for the rest of that week, relaying messages when she needed them, making sure Simon didn't try to contact her again using a different number. He did, twice, but she didn't need to know that. Listening to his begging, his insistence on her attention, I realized that yes, Simon still wanted her. He wanted her back in his life because she'd always made things easier for him. I deleted his pathetic, whining messages, which were all the same. *I need you. I'm suffering. Help me.*

As fucked up as I was, I never used Chere in the selfish way that Simon used Chere. I gave back to her in whatever ways I could. *I'm better than him. I'm better.* Simon Baldwin was a low bar to measure myself against as a boyfriend and lover, but I was trying. I wanted to get better.

Simon wants to get better too.

But hell, he needed to do that for himself. He'd taken enough from Chere, and it wasn't her business or my business if his life was starting to fall apart again. I felt secure in this line of reasoning until late Sunday night, when Andrew sent a barrage of texts.

Chere was drifting to sleep beside me when her phone started vibrating on my side table. "Is that Andrew?" she asked with a half-smile. Her friend texted her a lot, about his work, or his relationship. He could be counted on to supply a vast stream of amusing minutiae. But these texts weren't amusing.

OMG BABES

JUST HEARD ABOUT SIMON

CHERE!!!!!

And I knew. I just knew.

"What's he saying?" she asked drowsily.

I didn't answer. I typed Simon's name into a search engine and watched the slew of headlines come up about his shaky sobriety and sudden overdose. Yahoo. CNN. Huffington Post. Twitter. #RIP #SIMONBALDWIN #TOOSOON

I sat up in bed, leaning over the phone. I had the craziest urge to destroy it, like that might make this go away. My next thought was, how do I hide these texts? How do I hide the fact that this has happened? But that would be impossible. Andrew would keep texting until Chere responded. If she didn't respond, he'd call, and if she didn't answer, he'd come over, because this was a big traumatic fucking deal and what the holy fuck was I going to do about this?

It was eleven o'clock at night. I looked down at Chere, almost asleep, and thought, I'll give myself one last night of peace before this shitstorm breaks wide. I texted back to Andrew, *Chere's sleeping. I don't want to wake her with this news. I'll tell her tomorrow.*

He didn't text back. I wondered if she told him that I'd barred her from helping Simon. I wondered if he blamed me for this. I knew Chere would blame me, even if Simon's fucking addiction problems weren't my fault.

* * * * *

I awakened before dawn in a pleasurable haze, with Price's fingers roving over my body. "I want you," he whispered.

It was still dark out. He was a shadow looming over me, stroking me, bringing my body to languorous life. His touch was bizarrely gentle, at least at first. He kissed me endlessly, pinching my nipples and tracing over my hips. It felt weird not to fight him, but there was no violence in his touch, just a possessive warmth.

He made me stretch my arms over my head, and then he kissed me everywhere. He went down on me, making me twist and jerk and whimper through two orgasms as dawn started to brighten the room. I peered down at him, drifting in pleasure. Was I dreaming? Had I died and gone to heaven? God, he was so good with his mouth. "Wow," I whispered. "Thank you."

"Shh."

He started kissing me again, running his fingers up and down my arm. His body felt hot against mine in the winter chill and I snuggled closer. His expression was strangely intense as he tipped my face up for another kiss.

Come inside me, please.

I wasn't allowed to issue demands, but I arched my hips against his thick, hard erection. His intent expression relaxed for a moment into a smile.

"I know you want it," he said in the half light. "You're always wet for me, beautiful girl."

I gazed into his blue eyes and spread my legs as he eased forward. He maintained the control, the careful facade for one or two strokes before he surged deep inside me. There was the violence I craved. He expelled a harsh breath and caught my lips in a smothering kiss. I spread my legs wider, letting him have me.

He squeezed my breasts and then his fingers crept up to my neck. He put his thumb and forefinger on either side of my windpipe, staring down at me. I waited for the inevitable loss of consciousness as I held his gaze. I knew I'd come back, and that he'd still be inside me and around me, and that this was just another form of control.

I reached to hold him as the edges of my vision turned black. I dreamed of wonderful things during the time I was out. Warmth and comfort, a fire, a blanket holding me safe and secure. I woke to the heady force of his possession. He kissed me and held my neck as I squeezed on his thick length. I wish I could describe how it felt to have him driving inside me. He was power and strength, and barely restrained force, and sometimes unexpected tenderness. He gripped my neck until we came together, gasping and arching toward each other, and he still held it afterward as he gazed down at me.

"Are you mine?" he asked.

"Yes, Sir."

"Are you happy being my slave?"

"Oh, yes, Sir."

He still looked unsettled. I traced his high Nordic cheekbones with my fingertips, trying to soothe him. He captured my fingers and brought them to his lips.

"We're lucky we found each other," he said after a moment, then drew out of me. We went into the bathroom, into his gargantuan shower, where we could continue to flirt and embrace. Sometimes Monday mornings could be wonderful.

"Chere," he said, while I was rinsing out my hair. "I have to tell you something. I don't want you to overreact. I don't want it to affect any of the things we just talked about, you know, that you're mine. That you belong to me. We're happy together, aren't we?"

I turned to him, watching the water sluice off his golden skin. *Price, I love you. I won't overreact.* I'd been waiting for us to have some kind of breakthrough, where he could admit that he saw a future between us. A marriage, a family. Maybe this was it. I prayed this was it...

"You can tell me anything," I said. "I'll always belong to you, no matter what."

I studied his expression. He didn't look like a man on the verge of professing eternal, undying love. I twisted the garnet ring around my finger and waited.

"Simon died last night," he said, holding my gaze. "According to the articles, he relapsed and suffered an overdose."

I stared at his face, at the hard, unforgiving planes of his nose and jaw. "What?"

He shut off the water in an abrupt movement and took me in his arms. "Don't overreact. Remember what we talked about. He's your past. You're not responsible for him."

"But..." My mind swam backward in horror to our meeting at my studio, and the texts Price hadn't allowed me to return. "He asked me for help. He said he was struggling."

"It's not your fault he lost that struggle."

But it felt like my fault. It felt like Price's fault. All the sex magic, all the marriage fantasies bled away in the face of this horrible news. I thought I should shove Price away from me, but before I could, he held me tighter.

"Don't," he said, staring down at me. "We're not going to lose our shit over this. You know the rule about Simon. It still stands. We're going to go to work, and concentrate on our lives, and move forward. Do you understand?"

I was having a little trouble catching my breath. He'd known this all morning. He'd known when he woke me up and had tender, hour-long sex with me. He'd known when he choked me out and brought me back with a kiss.

"When did this happen?" I asked, but what I really meant was, *How long have you known, and why are you only telling me now?*

"I found out last night. Andrew texted last night."

"I want my phone back." I needed some control back, because this was fucked up. Our rule about Simon? Really? Simon was dead, possibly because I'd turned my back on him, and Price was stuck on our goddamn rule. Tears rose in my eyes. Simon was *dead*. Overdosed.

"Don't flip out about this," he said, handing me a towel. "You know what will happen if you flip out on me. Let's give it some time to process. We'll talk about it tonight, okay?"

"Can I have my phone back?"

"Tonight. After we talk."

How could he be so calm? Didn't he understand he was implicated in Simon's tragic death? Tonight seemed a thousand years away, and yet I never wanted tonight to come. I dreaded it. I dreaded the furious, unguarded things I'd say to Price about this, and the things he'd do to me in return. I dreaded everything, and Simon...

It was too late for Simon. I should have helped him, and now it was too fucking late.

* * * * *

I entered my studio feeling numb. Maybe I was in shock. Simon was an ex, yes. He'd done awful things to me, yes, but we'd spent ten years together and maybe I'd owed him something, some basic human decency and caring. Maybe I could have prevented his death.

I hunched over my computer, wondering if Price was watching me. He'd refused to show me where the camera was, or how many there were, and I accepted that because I was his slave and I pretty much allowed him to do whatever the fuck he wanted for some reason that made no sense to me now. We had a rule, and that rule was that I could have nothing to do with Simon.

I broke that rule and put Simon's name into a search engine. I clicked the News tab and was confronted by an endless barrage of morbid headlines about his overdose. His dark eyes stared out at me from beneath black shaggy hair in the photos. *Why didn't you help?*

I read the first few articles, mostly accounts of his life, his talent, the loss to the art world. I learned the heartbreaking details of how he'd died in a nightclub bathroom, seizing on the cold, hard tile. Once he stopped, he lay there for over an hour because the other clubgoers thought he was only passed out. He'd stuck a needle in his arm, unable to maintain another moment of sobriety.

I wondered what he'd thought of at that moment. I wondered if he'd felt guilt or regret, or just relief to be getting high again. Maybe he wanted to die. With the stuff he used, it was only a matter of time. *Bad high,* an anonymous witness had offered in an interview. *Strong shit has been going around the city, and Simon Baldwin never knew when to stop.*

I closed out the articles and tried to work, but the metal swam before my vision as I wiped away tears. I tried to pull it together for my two PM meeting with Vinod, but he noticed my red eyes.

"What has happened, my dear?" he asked.

"A death. A tragic one. I lost an old friend."

I left it at that, because if I said any more, all the grief and guilt and furious angst would vomit out of me like lava onto the sample display between us. At least Vinod seemed pleased with the jewelry I'd designed, and after a few kind words of condolence, he left me alone with my thoughts.

The problem was, I didn't know what to do with my thoughts. I stewed and read more articles, and cried again, and hoped Price wouldn't visit me. He didn't. At least he allowed me some sexual space on this day. If he'd come to me and demanded a blowjob in the back room, what would I have done? Could I have said no? I started to question why I let Price control me the way he did. He said it was for my own good, for my protection, and most of the time I liked it, but someone had *died*, and now, suddenly, the control felt out of control.

Finally, I put my work away and took the elevator up to the offices of Eriksen Architectural Design. I wasn't sure of my mission, only that I had to see Price and talk to him about what had happened. I needed him to admit that he'd fucked up, that he'd steered me wrong and was at fault in this. Esther greeted me at the reception desk.

"Chere! How are things? I haven't seen you in a while."

"Things are great." I managed a smile only because I needed it to get what I wanted. "Is Mr. Eriksen here?"

"He's in a meeting."

"I need to talk to him."

Her smile faded. She stood as if to stop me, but I was already heading down the hall to the back.

"What— What do you need to talk to him about?" she asked, scurrying after me. "He just sat down with some new clients."

"In the conference room?"

"Chere, wait."

I wasn't waiting. I didn't want to get Esther in trouble, but I couldn't fucking wait any more. I reached the conference room door and swung it open. Familiar faces looked up at me. Jennifer was there, and Praneesh, and some faces I didn't know, presumably the clients. Praneesh and Jennifer smiled, surprised. The clients watched me in expectation, as if I was simply a late associate. But Price's face...

He looked right at me, his chin propped on steepled fingers. His expression said *Don't do it. Don't dare.*

"We're in a meeting," he said. "I'll see you later this evening."

I glared at him. "I need to see you now."

The smiles at the table faded, replaced by uneasy glances between the big boss man in his power suit, and me, the interloper flushed with emotional anger. Price pushed back in his chair and nodded to the clients.

"Please, continue. I'll return in a moment."

He left it to Jennifer and Praneesh to explain who I was to the other suits in the room. He took my elbow and led me down the hall to his office.

"Are you out of your fucking mind?" he asked. His voice was as tight as his grip on my elbow.

"Yes, I think I am," I began, ready to pitch into a diatribe.

"Wait. Not in the hall."

He steered me into his office and shut the door behind us. I turned to him, seething with all the hot, awful conflict that had propelled me over here in the middle of the day, in the middle of his meeting. He yanked me to him and kissed me. One of his knuckles stroked my cheek.

"No," I said.

"Why not?" His arm slid around me, hard and muscled through his civilized suit. "You said you needed me, that you couldn't wait." He groped my ass and started yanking up my skirt. "Sometimes I don't want to wait either."

"No, I don't want this. I need to talk to you."

I pushed at him but he only held me harder. The caressing knuckle turned to long fingers gripping my cheek. He kissed me again, not soft now, but commanding and angry. I felt trapped within his power, within his enveloping scent and large body. I'd be lost in a moment. We'd be fucking on his desk, and nothing else would matter. I lifted my hands between us and shoved for everything I was worth.

"I said no," I yelled. I backed away, holding out my arms to ward him off. "Don't touch me."

I expected hotter anger in reply, but he seemed to have discharged it with the kiss. He looked bored now, haughty, maybe a little bemused that I'd pushed him away from me. He pursed his lips and adjusted one of his cuff links. They weren't my design.

"What do you want?" he asked. "Why are you here? I'm busy."

"You know why I'm here. We need to talk."

"About what?"

"About Simon," I said, my voice rising again. "About what happened to Simon, and your part in it. My part in it."

"There are no parts to anything. Your ex was a fucking drug addict. He died."

His cool, uncaring tone made me grit my teeth. "That's it? That's your final word on the matter?"

"Yes, that's my final word, which you very well fucking know." He crossed his arms over his chest. "What happened to him has nothing to do with either one of us. He's not in either one of our lives. He's *not going to be.*"

"But he is. Just because you insist he's not, doesn't make it true."

"If he's in our lives, it's because you're fucking up." He stared down into my face, then turned and walked across his office, over by the window. "Jesus, Chere. Do you still love him?"

"No, but—"

"Then why the fuck do you care? Why do you care so much?"

"Why *don't* you care? He died, Price."

He threw up his arms. "What did you think was going to happen? He used heroin and crystal meth, and crack, and God knows what else. He was an addict, full stop. He was a fuck up."

"I fucking know that."

"Then what do you want from me? Do you want me to cry for your fucked up, abusive ex-boyfriend? Do you want me to throw myself on the ground and tear at my hair and say it was all my fault because I wouldn't let you go to him? What do you think you could have done for him?"

"I don't know! Something!"

"Nothing. There's nothing you could have done."

"You didn't even let me try."

"Because I knew it would end this way. And you would have been involved with him again, and you would have been hurt again, and blaming yourself now instead of me. Or did you think you might have been able change him?" His smile was a mocking grimace. "Do you think he would have fallen in love with you again, you and your golden fucking pussy? You probably wanted that."

"I didn't!"

"Oh, you could have made him straighten the fuck up, right? Because you're magical."

"We loved each other once," I shouted. I felt hurt and humiliated, all my feelings belittled. "Simon hit me, yes, he used me, but at least he let me live my life and be myself. He allowed me to have normal human emotions like concern and anger and grief."

"Because he made you have those emotions every single fucking day, and he would have done it again if you got involved with him. He *did* do it again! This is all happening because you let him in the door of your fucking studio." His expression was awful. His gaze burned me. "Are you seriously grieving over his death? What the fuck for? He never loved you. He used you and hurt you. God, Chere, what's wrong with you? Why can't you fucking *remember*?" The tortured words echoed off the glass walls of his office, resonating between us. There was a faint knock at the door.

"Not now," he said. "I'll be there in a minute."

His voice was strident enough to send the timid knocker away. He turned back to me, the bright glare from the window outlining his powerful frame, and glinting in his blond hair.

"I don't give a flying fuck about Simon Baldwin's death. I don't care," he said. "What I care about is you being safe and protected—"

"Protected? You keep saying you're protecting me, but you don't care about anything but your own interests!" He stalked toward me, but I kept talking, spitting out words. "You're jealous of Simon, jealous of anyone who has a part of me. You want everything. You want me all to yourself."

"We both know that! We both agreed to that. I earned you, you little bitch. You're mine." He grabbed my hand and showed me the ring on my finger. "You wear my collar, you live in my house, you belong to me." He snaked an arm around my waist and pulled me roughly against him. "And you know how that goes, starshine. I decide who you have in your life. I decide who you help, and who helps you."

"Let go of me." I struggled in his grasp, but he only held me tighter.

"I'm never letting you go. I told you that at the beginning."

"But someone *died*," I shrieked. "Someone died, and it makes me crazy that you don't even care."

"I don't care because he was an asshole who hurt you." He shook me until my eyes met his. "I don't care because you were always meant to belong to me, and Simon was always meant to flatline in a fucking nightclub bathroom, and you need to fucking get over your emotional victim bullshit."

I slapped him. Hard. When he didn't react, I launched myself at him, scratching and flailing. We struggled until he caught my hands in his. The arrogant nonchalance had left his face.

"Are you finished?" he asked.

"Yes, I'm finished with you."

His whole body tensed. He looked really big when he was angry. "You're wrong about that," he said, his blue eyes pale and cold as ice. "When this fucking tantrum is over, you'll still be mine. Remember that."

I shivered at his tone, and subsided in his grasp. I couldn't bear to think about a future between us, much less the repercussions of this confrontation.

"This conversation is over," he said. "I have to go back to my meeting. I have work to do."

I stared at him in befuddled silence. He had to go back to his meeting. Nothing I had said to him mattered, nothing about my feelings or my emotional pain managed to permeate his armor of control. *You need to fucking get over your emotional victim bullshit.*

He claimed to care, but he didn't fucking care. I pulled out of his arms and ran away from him, because I needed some space to breathe. I left his office, ran down the hall and through the lobby, and out into the corridor toward the elevators. I listened as I ran, straining to hear if he was coming behind me. That was when I realized I wasn't looking for a place to breathe. I was looking for a place to hide.

CHAPTER TWELVE: CONTROL

I didn't expect her to leave the building. I didn't expect her to literally *go*, but when I went back to the meeting and switched on the feed to her studio camera, she wasn't there. I kept watching, but she didn't show up. And didn't show up. And didn't show up.

She'd left.

I resolved not to panic. She was in slave revolt mode, which sometimes happened. I finished out the meeting and went home, and waited for her there. Nothing. She didn't come home. Of course, I'd never given back her goddamned phone, so I couldn't call her. My mind ran in circles, hot anger mixed with regret. She'd left me. I knew she'd do it eventually. Now I had to figure out how to bring her back, because Simon wasn't going to be the one to steal her from me, especially from the grave.

When eight o'clock arrived with no Chere, I texted Andrew.

Is Chere at your place?

No, he texted back.

But he was an idiot, because if she wasn't at his place, he would have texted something appropriately dramatic like OMG WHAT HAPPENED or OMG IS SHE LOST?

I had to go get her. She was wrought up. I understood that, but rules were fucking rules and she couldn't just blow up in my face and run away to her friend's house. I took a cab to Andrew and Craig's building and helped a woman with her grocery bags in order to get through the door. I walked down the hall and knocked on the door of 24B.

Andrew answered with a pout on his face, and his arms crossed over his chest. "She's not here."

"I know she's here."

I pushed past him into the living room. Craig stood up from his place on the couch, but didn't greet me.

"I need to talk to her," I said.

"I don't think she wants to talk to you," said Andrew. "In fact, she told me to give you this. She doesn't want it anymore."

He held out her garnet ring. Fuck. I wasn't shocked that she'd taken it off, but it wasn't staying off, not if I had anything to say about it. I shoved it in my pocket.

"Is she in the back?" I moved toward the hallway, but Andrew jumped in front of me, his skinny arms held out, his lips pursed in a stubborn line.

"She doesn't want to see you. Aren't you listening? She needs some time."

I stared at him, at his wild, blond, curly hair and his childishly innocent features. Cute kid, trying to play the hero. The protector. His boyfriend hovered in the background, doing some protecting of his own. Both of them were good guys, but they weren't going to keep me from retrieving my runaway.

"I know you're her friend," I said calmly. "I understand that you want to help, but the best thing to do right now is to let us talk."

"Talk?" His frown deepened. "When do you two ever talk? You give orders, and she obeys."

"Yes, that's the way we work," I retorted. "You understand about us, about our dynamic—"

"No, I don't understand. I don't get why you treat her like a dog on a leash, like a child who needs to have every aspect of her life micromanaged."

"Andy, hon," said Craig. "This isn't your fight."

"It *is* my fight. Because he—" He pointed angrily in my direction. "He's taken all the fight out of Chere. You saw how she was when she got here."

"She was upset because we argued," I said. "We just need some time to work things out."

"No, you're going to leave her alone."

I raised my eyebrows at him, to no avail. Damn toppy subs.

"Chere's my best friend," he said, sticking out his chin. "If she won't speak up for herself, then I'm going to speak on her behalf."

I sighed and rubbed my forehead, because I had to listen. It was that, or beat up a twenty-two year old gay kid wearing a lavender scrunchie, and I already had a police record from beating up Simon last year.

"If this is about the thing with Chere's ex—" I began.

"No. It's about more than Simon's overdose. This is about all your rules and consequences. This is about the fact that you monitor my texts to Chere, and take away her phone whenever you want. This is about Chere and I having to hang out at the Big Apple Diner because I'm not allowed to be alone with her anywhere else. I mean, what the fuck?"

"Every relationship has rules."

"Yes, but most relationships also have freedom, and consideration for the other person's feelings. Most relationships involve some fucking trust. She used to love you."

"She still loves me!"

He shook his head. "She's lost faith in you. She told me so when she got here, that you don't care about her, that you only care about yourself."

"That's not true."

"Oh, I believe you care about her," he said, looking me up and down. "I believe you love her, but you need to think about how you show it, because from the outside, your relationship looks majorly fucked up. To me, from the outside..." He faltered, then persisted. "To tell the brutal truth, you come off like a desperate, cowardly man. The way you behave toward her—"

"Cowardly?" I interrupted. The word felt disgusting in my throat. "Cowardly?"

I heard Craig shift as I raised my voice, but Andrew didn't back down. "Yes, cowardly. You're afraid of losing her, so afraid of losing her that you're scaring her away. She showed up here scared out of her mind. I only just got her calmed down."

"Scared? Scared of what?"

"Of your jealousy! What would it have hurt, to let her try to help Simon?"

"It would have hurt Chere."

I was shouting now. Craig came closer and held out a quelling hand. "Can both of you calm down? We have neighbors."

"I care about her," I said to Andrew. I worked hard to modulate my voice. I had to get my shit together. I had to be the strong one, so I could get Chere home and calmed down, and get us out of this fucking mess. "As for the rules, she agreed to every one of them."

"Of course she did. She's a submissive, and a masochist. She's never going to put the brakes on. Believe me, I know the mindset, but your job is to—"

"To keep her safe. To keep her out of the hands of users and abusers."

Andrew glared at me. No, it wasn't a glare, exactly. It was a stare. Craig stared at me too, and then, like a lightning strike, I got it. They thought *I* was a user and abuser. They thought *I* was a threat to Chere. Not Simon Baldwin. Me, the man who had saved her from that relationship and given her my love at great fucking risk to my peace and sanity.

"I've never abused her," I said, my voice rough with roiling anger. "I have never, ever abused her. Everything between us is consensual. Everything I do, everything I say, every rule, every protocol, every session between us is motivated by my fucking love for her. I guide her. I encourage her. I write her fucking poetry."

"If you love her, why do you hold her so hard? You control everything in her life." Andrew said it like it was a bad thing. Like it wasn't what she'd begged for that day in my dungeon a few months ago.

"You don't understand us." I waved a hand at him, waved off all his misguided, meddling-best-friend bullshit. "I need to talk to Chere. She needs to come home. It's late." I made another move toward the hall. Andrew didn't budge. Motherfucker.

"She's not going anywhere if she doesn't want to."

"She's coming home with me tonight if I have to pick her up and drag her out of here," I informed him. "And you and Craig aren't going to fucking stop me. I'm sorry, but you're not."

He ruffled up. "I'll call the police if I have to."

"Andrew, it's okay."

Her voice materialized first, and then she was there, a miserable angel drifting out of the darkness. I wanted to go to her and hold her, but Andrew still stood in the way. She put her hands on his shoulders and turned him to face her.

"Thanks for sticking up for me," she said, pressing her cheek to his. "You've been so brave, but I think you've done enough."

He shook his head. "I haven't done enough. I've been too quiet about...about this." He gestured toward me, the evil user and abuser who couldn't be named.

"Chere, we need to go home," I said, staring at her very intently. "We have things to discuss."

She didn't look happy to see me, or happy at the idea of coming home with me. She looked tired. "It's okay," she told Andrew again. "He's right. We have things to talk about. This is something I need to work out on my own."

"But I don't know..." He stopped, clutching her hand. "I don't know if you can. Remember...?"

Remember Simon? That other abuser you got tangled up with for ten years? It was all I could do not to pummel him. I was nothing like Simon. In fact, I was the opposite of Simon. Simon had never cared for Chere, and I...

Well. Maybe Andrew had a point. Maybe I cared about her too much, to the point where I exerted unhealthy levels of monitoring and control. Well, I'd warned her. It always came back to that. I'd warned her what I would be like, and she'd agreed. I'd told her that if she ran away from me, I'd bring her back whether she wanted it or not. I knew she was remembering that now.

"It's going to be okay," I said, and I was talking to her, not Andrew. I wanted her to understand I wasn't going to take her home and explode. I was going to take her home and fix what had gone wrong between us. If I could build bridges and skyscrapers, I could fix a faltering relationship. *There's always a way...*

She gave Andrew a long hug and stepped away from him, back into my control. We didn't touch each other. There was too much tension. I followed her to the door as Andrew watched with a doom-and-gloom gaze. He was a nice kid, but he didn't have a clue about Chere and me, and our dynamic. He needed to butt out and let us work through our own complicated shit.

"Are you going to punish me?" Chere asked when we were almost to the car. She sounded a bit snarky, but mostly terrified, which touched something in my heart. Despite her fear, her vulnerability, she'd agreed to put herself back in my hands.

"I'm not going to punish you," I said, because I knew that would be the wrong tack. "Simon doesn't deserve any more of your pain. I'm going to re-train you instead. Take a few days and go back over what it means to belong to someone. Do you think that would be helpful?"

She only hesitated a moment before she answered. "Yes, Sir. That would probably help."

* * * * *

Was I crazy to go back to him? Maybe. Andrew thought so, but in my heart, I wanted re-training. I wanted peace. I wanted my brain to go silent, and Price was great at making that happen. From the moment we got home, he was in Master mode, giving me no choice but to surrender.

He put on my collar as soon as we got home, and put me through my paces in the dungeon, doling out pain on the spanking bench, the rack, the sawhorse—though not the painful, pussy-torturing side of the sawhorse. He lectured me about submission as he carried out various torments, but he wasn't angry and rough the way he sometimes was when I'd pissed him off. He was...thoughtful. Andrew had pretty much accused him of abusing me, and maybe that factored into this careful, deliberate form of training. Once he'd broken down my body, he turned my attention to his needs and desires as my Master. *Kneel. Kiss. Back straight. Open your mouth. Suck me.*

I didn't get any pleasure or orgasms myself, but I hadn't expected to. When it was time for bed, he got out the chastity belt, plugged me and strapped me in for the night. The lesson was obvious, even without his punctilious reminders: All my lust and attention was to be centered on him.

After that, he locked me into the manacles, and used rope to secure my wrists to his headboard so I couldn't so much as turn over without him knowing it.

"Neither one of us is going to work for the rest of this week," he informed me as he slid into bed beside me and took me in his arms. "You're going to spend the next few days naked and on your knees. Do you understand why?"

"Yes, Sir," I whispered, leaning my head on his shoulder. "Thank you. I want to belong to you." I wasn't just babbling what I thought he wanted to hear. I was babbling my real, true feelings, because the bitter truth was that I found security in being his slave. Anger, frustration, and panic bled away when I handed him the control, and the next couple days felt a lot like the first few days I'd spent in his home: strenuous but deeply rewarding.

In the beginning it had been hard to find the slavey side of myself, but now it was easier, like relaxing into a familiar bed after a long and trying day. I still felt guilty about Simon's death, but I could process that later, when I could get some distance and perspective. The funeral was Thursday afternoon, near the end of this re-training odyssey, and maybe that would be the best time to deal with my pent-up feelings. If Simon's funeral didn't bring me peace, it would at least deliver some closure on that chapter of my life.

God, I hoped so, because Price was my future, and Simon needed to become my past for that to work. I understood all of this, even as Price went on and on about forward progress and self-respect during sessions over the spanking bench. *You're not that woman any more. You weren't happy then. Your life was tied up in regrets and shame. I want you to let go of your past mistakes and reach your true potential. I want you to be happy.*

Of course, he said this while he applied horribly painful clamps to my nipples, and whipped me, and sodomized me three times a day with miserly amounts of lube so it wouldn't feel too good.

Re-training. Punishment. In the end, they were pretty much the same thing.

At least there was poetry. He wrote me some poetry the next day, and then set me to reading some of his favorite poets while he called in to work meetings. Byron, Eliot, Whitman, Browning, Neruda in both English and Spanish. I didn't do any work for those days, aside from serving him, but design ideas flowed as I stroked over every line, slope, and plane of my Master's body. I came up with concepts for new pieces, now that my mind was clearer and free of damned emotional clutter.

I belonged to Price. He loved me. It was so simple and safe and warm. He was concerned about me and wanted me to reach my true potential. I wanted to be happy because I knew that would make him happy, and nothing made me happier than my Master's pleased smile.

I was tired by mid-week, and a little sore, but it all seemed worth it because things felt normal again, and there wasn't a bunch of anger and tension standing between us. Then Thursday came, and I brought up Simon's funeral.

Of course, it had crossed my mind that he might not want me to attend, but I figured I'd explain about rituals and closure, and he'd come to acknowledge my need to say goodbye. I imagined he might even insist on attending with me, so he could stand beside me and hold my hand through the most difficult parts, perhaps even brush away my tears.

All of this was so far removed from the reality of what happened, it might have been poetry in his leather-bound books.

"Do you really think it's a good idea to go?" he asked, looking down at me. I was the supplicant, posed on my knees as he lounged on the couch.

"I think I have to go," I said, as respectfully as I could.

"Oh, you *have* to go." His arched brow and curt intonation told me this conversation was about to go awry. "I'm surprised you'd say that, after everything we've talked about this week."

"I know, Sir. I know it's my past, but that's exactly why I need to go. I need to move on. I need closure."

"Yes, you do need closure." He reached to stroke my hair, a gentle gesture that belied the storm brewing in his eyes. "But I don't think a PR-designed art world funeral is the place to find it."

"Where then?"

"How about inside you? How about letting this go? How about forgiving yourself for this crime you never committed? If you go to that funeral, I know what you're going to do." He yanked up my chin when I tried to look away. "I know you, Chere. You're going to whip yourself bloody, enumerating your many faults until every crying poser and art freak there is a victim of your negligence. Or mine. It'll be my fault, right? The whole thing. The whole funeral," he said, waving his hand. "My fault for not letting you help poor Simon face his self-inflicted demons."

"This has nothing to do with you," I said, and that was my fatal mistake, but I barged on anyway. "This is between me and a person I had a relationship with. If I feel guilt— If I wished I'd helped—"

"It wouldn't have changed anything!"

"I could have done it though, even without your permission. And if I want to feel guilty about that, and go pay my last respects, I don't see why you won't let me do it. Why does it matter to you?"

"Your last respects," he said in a biting tone. "The funeral's going to be a joke, some last ditch effort to sanitize his legacy. It's going to be a lot of people wanting to be seen, wanting to rub shoulders with the art world players."

"So what if it is?"

"And everyone there will be culpable for the train wreck that was Simon Baldwin, not just you. There's no honor in that, no respect. It'll be a pack of fucking users pretending they cared for a waste of a person."

"A waste of a person?" I choked on the harsh phrase. "Simon touched a lot of lives. His art made a lot of people happy. It's in homes and museums all over the world. A hundred years from now—"

"Don't." His voice was steel, hard, a cold threat as we faced off against each other. "Don't tell me he's wonderful. Don't tell me Simon is some shining beacon of humanity that we must remember."

"I want to remember him. Just me, for personal reasons." God, I didn't even know anymore what those personal reasons were, or why it was so important for me to go. I just needed Price to allow me to make this decision. Otherwise I had no personal power at all. "Let me do this, please. Give me this last chance. What does it matter to you?" I said again, stupidly blundering into my own destruction.

"Jesus Christ," he said, pulling me up from the floor. "I thought I'd explained why it mattered. I thought we'd been over this enough times."

But we weren't over it. I wanted to go to Simon's funeral, and the man in front of me wasn't going to let me go, and I was a prisoner here, naked, vulnerable, powerless, and I didn't want to be a slave anymore, and *fuck, fuck, fuck,* he was dragging me toward the dungeon, and I couldn't stop him even though I fought with every ounce of my strength.

"Let me go," I pleaded, and I didn't know if I meant *Let me go to the funeral* or simply *Let go of my arm.*

Either way, he wasn't listening, and I wasn't strong enough to break free of his control.

CHAPTER THIRTEEN: SUFFOCATION

I'd told her she wouldn't always like being under my control, that she wouldn't always be happy, and she wasn't happy now.

Bang.

She was in the cage, and she was trying to get out of it.

Bang.

She'd been trying for a couple of hours.

Bang. Bang. BANG.

"Shut the fuck up," I yelled. "I've had enough of the fucking noise."

I'd put a gag on her, but she took it off. She screamed and swore, demanding that I let her go. After our peaceful, productive week of training, all hell had broken loose because I wouldn't let her go to that goddamn funeral. Fuck. All I'd wanted was to spend a quiet afternoon with my slave at my feet.

"Let me out," she screamed.

I stood beside the cage watching her, not just for safety's sake, but because I'd never seen her lose her shit to this degree. And it was over *Simon.* Fuck, she made me so furious. Didn't she understand? This damn funeral would just cause more pointless emotional trauma.

"Let me out. I want out!"

The metallic sound of the bars rattled my nerves every time she flung herself against them. In between flailing, she kicked, *bang, bang, bang.*

"Give me a safe word," she pleaded. "I need a safe word. I'm missing the funeral, damn you. It started at three o'clock."

"You're not going. That's why you're in the cage. I told you that you weren't allowed to go."

"*Let me ouuuttt!*"

"And the fact that you're still in there kicking and screaming—"

She went nuts again, banging her feet so hard against the bars that the metal strained. It wouldn't break. I'd studied engineering along with architecture. I knew the cage would hold. I also knew that we were engaged in the battle of all battles, and that she needed to calm down.

"I want out," she cried, looking up at me. "This isn't a game. I'm not playing anymore."

"It was never a game," I said tightly. "Is that what you thought? That we were just 'playing?' That you weren't really my slave?"

"I don't want to be your slave anymore." She buried her face in her hands. Her hair was a tangled mess.

I crouched down beside the cage, just out of hitting and scratching reach. "You want Simon, is that it?"

"Yes!"

I sighed and prayed for calm, and somehow refrained from pointing out, again, that her fucking ex-boyfriend was fucking dead, and that she needed to get over it. I understood about mourning and regret, but they hadn't been together in years now, and he represented everything ugly in her past existence.

"I don't want this anymore," she said. "I don't want your control anymore."

"Is that true? Or is that only how you feel in this moment, because I'm not letting you do what you want?"

She made a sound like she'd kill me if she had the chance. "I want you to give me some space, Price. This once, just this once, let me have my way."

"No."

"Oh God. I hate you," she screamed, rattling the bars again. "I'm safewording."

"You don't have a safe word."

"I want you to let me go. I want you to stop being my Master." She said something else that was eclipsed by sobs. I tugged a lock of her hair through the bars.

"I'm not keeping you in this cage as your Master. I'm doing it as a friend. As someone who cares about you. Simon—"

"Stop talking about Simon. Don't you dare fucking talk to me about Simon ever again. I trusted you. I returned to you and went through this fucking re-training bullshit. I sucked your dick four times yesterday. Let me out!"

God, the screaming. I thought she'd calm down after a while and listen to reason. I thought she'd remember that she belonged to me, and see the wisdom in staying with me instead of going to some shitshow funeral.

"Let me out of here, damn it! I'm not kidding. I'm finished, Price. I want out. I want out! Please, I'll lose my mind if you don't let me out."

"Out of the cage, or out of our relationship?"

She kicked the bars again, brutal anger and frustration. "What do you fucking think?"

"I think you need to pull your fucking shit together. When this is over—"

"It's never going to be over." She rolled over and crouched on her knees, and glared out at me. "Don't you see? You're always going to be this way. A selfish, jealous, insecure, abusive prick. You're holding me prisoner against my will." With each word, she shook the bars. On the last three, she rattled them hard, snapping my nerves. "Against my will. Do you understand that? I don't want to be here. This is not consensual."

She'd taken her collar off a long time ago, before I gagged her, before she took the gag off too, in blatant disregard for the rules. The rules didn't matter now, though. She was rejecting our relationship, rejecting everything about it. Rejecting me.

"Is he worth this?" I shouted at her. "Is he worth destroying everything between us? All our history, everything we've built?"

"You destroyed it," she shouted back. "It was just a fucking funeral, the only chance I had to say goodbye. What's wrong with you? Is your jealousy that wide and that deep? How fucking psychotic do you have to be—"

"Watch your fucking mouth!"

"I won't watch my fucking mouth, Master." She said *Master* in a mocking tone and banged the bars again. "How fucking psycho do you have to be to keep someone away from a fucking funeral?"

"From Simon Baldwin's funeral," I said, and now I was the one banging the bars. "From the funeral of a man who fucked you up, who took your money, who hit you, who punched you, who cheated on you. You hid from him. You barricaded yourself behind deadbolts. Remember that? I remember. Why don't you remember? You were fucking there."

I stood outside myself and watched as I shouted at a naked, raging woman in a cage. I could put the princess in the tower. Any rich fucking prince, or prick, could do that. It didn't mean I could keep her. She accused me of jealousy and abuse because I wouldn't let her attend her abuser's funeral. Fuck my life. The abuse label, after all this time, after all the care I'd taken to avoid it.

She didn't understand, she didn't care, and she didn't love me. I knew it would end up this way. I always fucking knew. I knew she'd turn on me, just like every other fucking woman in my past.

"If you don't stop kicking the fucking cage—" I began.

"You'll what? What will you do to me that you haven't already done?"

I'll leave you. No, I'd already done that. Twice.

I'll hurt you. No, I did that just about every day.

I'll let you go. There. That was something I hadn't done yet. My hands curled into fists as a trembling vortex of loss opened inside me, in my gut and my chest and shoulders and all the way up to my brain.

I'll let you go, Chere, because I don't know what else to do, where else to take this fucking debacle we call our relationship.

Simon's funeral was over by now. I couldn't go back and change my mind, and let her go, even if I wanted to. I couldn't make her un-hate me, not this time. She was safewording out, bang by bang, kick by kick against the metal bars that were supposed to keep her safe.

But relationships, real, healthy relationships weren't supposed to be like this. *Good girl, Chere. You know you can do better than this. Better than me. You've always been a fighter, you scrappy little bitch.*

But approving of her choices didn't mean I was happy about them. No, I wanted to snatch up the cage with her inside and throw it against the fucking wall.

"Shut up," I yelled. "Shut the fuck up for one fucking minute and listen to me."

"No." She put her hands over her ears. "Let me out. Let me out!"

"Jesus fucking shit." I rubbed my fingers down my forehead, over my eyes and down my cheeks. I didn't want to let her go. I'd put so much time into our relationship. So much physical and emotional energy. Why? Why had I tried when I knew all along it would eventually fail?

I forced myself to reach for the lock. I opened it, hard, angrily. "You want out? Then come the fuck out, you fucking piece of shit." I called her a piece of shit. I think I really meant me.

I kicked open the door, my mouth pursed in a furious line. She stopped flailing against the bars and crouched on her knees, staring out at me.

"Come on," I said. "You wanted out. The door's open."

"You go away first. I'm not coming out until you go away. I don't want you to touch me."

"Get out of my cage."

"I'm serious. I don't want you to touch me." Her voice cracked. She was crying. "I don't want you to touch me ever again."

"I'm not going to touch you. Get the fuck out. Get out of my dungeon, get out of my house, get out of my fucking life and save both of us a lot of trouble." I pointed toward the door. "You have one hour to get the fuck out of this apartment and never come back."

She crawled from the cage and headed for the door without a glance in my direction. I wasn't even sure she heard what I'd said, heard my shouted permission. She was leaving either way. I could see it in her movements, in the wary way she fled for the exit.

Fuck.

Slavery shouldn't end this way. A relationship like ours, that had been so close and so connected, shouldn't end this way. But facts were facts. I couldn't give her the relationship she wanted. I felt too emotionally decimated to try.

Instead I sat on the floor by the cage and looked at my watch as the minutes ticked by. She'd be getting dressed now, hurriedly, throwing her things into her suitcases, if she even took the time to do that. She'd run outside and flag down a cab, and scurry to Andrew's. At least there was that. At least she had a safe place to go, someone trustworthy to take her in.

Damn me to hell. Fuck. I'd only ever wanted to take care of her. Why was it beyond me? I'd designed mile-long bridges across vast bodies of water, and yet I couldn't bridge a body's width of distance between me and her.

I'm never leaving you, never. I remembered when she'd said that. I remembered how comforted it made me feel. Lies and empty promises. "You're just another fake slave," I muttered in the heavy silence. "Another woman out to use me for money and power."

I knew that wasn't true, but I had to say it, or else admit the actual truth, that I was the one who couldn't make our shit work. Otherwise I had to admit that I was the one with the fucked up past, that I was the one who was weak and haunted by past relationships. I was the one who was an unfixable mess.

An hour and a half passed before I finally did what I'd wanted to do. I stood and threaded my fingers through the bars of the cage, picked it up and flung it against the wall hard enough to leave jagged gouges in the concrete. The cage bounced off the wall and fell sideways. The violence felt satisfying, yes.

But it didn't feel good.

"Chere," I yelled.

I turned my head, listening for any sound that she was still in the apartment. Nothing. I walked out into my room, then down the hall to the guest room. Empty. She was gone, along with a couple of her suitcases.

Fuck me. She'd done exactly what I told her to do.

* * * * *

"Can you...? Do you have...?" I tried to pull myself together. "I need a room for a while. Is the tenth floor corner room overlooking the park available?"

The woman at the Gramercy Park Hotel desk blinked at me, then looked down and tapped some keys on her computer.

"It appears to be available. How long will you be checking in?"

"I don't know."

She looked dubious. I didn't blame her. I was so freaked out and messed up in the head right now that I couldn't even bring myself to go to Andrew's. I'd thrown on mismatched clothes and packed everything so quickly that my luggage was bursting at the seams. I'd cried off my makeup, and my hair was so messed up I could feel it. A silent porter in a pristine uniform stood beside me anyway, ready to help me upstairs.

"I'm not sure how long I'm staying. Can we take it day by day?" I fished in my wallet for a credit card. I had the money to stay here. I'd already received payments from some celebrity clients, and I got gargantuan monthly checks from Vinod, now that my jewelry was for sale in his vast network of boutiques. I made a monthly income from renting my apartment, and Price never let me pay for anything.

Price.

Shit. Don't think about him now.

"We can put your card on file," said the woman. "If you would be kind enough to give us twenty-four hours notice before you plan to check out?"

"Uh, yeah. Sure. I can do that."

I just needed to go upstairs. I needed to wash my face and take a bath. I needed food. I needed to figure out what I was going to do next in my fucked up life.

A few moments later, I was headed toward the elevator, with the porter trailing a luggage cart behind me. *Tenth floor, corner room.*

The Gramercy Park Hotel was the first place I thought of when I realized I couldn't go to Andrew's. It wasn't just my emotional state that kept me from running there. It was that Price would look there first, and I didn't want to be found yet. I also didn't want Andrew and Craig to be drawn into all our drama.

No, this was my problem to fix, my life to reboot. I didn't know how yet, or when, or why. Hell, I could barely string two thoughts together. At least I had my phone back, swiped from Price's nightstand. I had my autonomy back, even if it was too late to make Simon's funeral.

Oh God, I needed to go somewhere and collapse. I needed to calm down. I needed to think.

Once the porter was gone, I stared at my stack of luggage and considered what I'd done. Well, I'd had to do it. He was crazy. He was pathologically unstable, or at least pathologically jealous and stubborn. But why had I come here?

I remembered the room like it was yesterday, remembered pushing open the door which he'd left slightly ajar. I remembered the lush velvet curtains and dark, heavy furniture. I remembered the sinking feeling when I'd seen his note lying on the bed.

I turned on more lights and perched on the edge of the sumptuous comforter. I'd come to our appointment at this exact time of day, but it had been summer. Lingering sun had fallen across this bed, shining on the replacement dress he'd left for me. He used to regularly destroy my clothes. That was back when I still wore clothes around him.

Fuck. What had I done? What had happened between us to make everything go so wrong?

I turned on my side and ran my fingers over the place he'd left the note. I remembered picking it up and walking to the window to read it in the evening light.

Good luck, starshine. That was all he'd written. I felt like I might die when I realized he'd left me with no name, no forwarding address. I remembered the crushing feeling of panic and betrayal.

It was important to come to this room and remember that moment when he'd abandoned me. It was important to recall that our relationship lacked trust from the very beginning. *It doesn't matter now*, I told myself. *It's over.* I picked up my phone and texted Andrew.

Are you there?

I'm here, he texted back. *Who's this?*

I was confused for a moment, but then I remembered that Price had had my phone all this time.

It's me, Chere, I wrote. *I have my phone back.*

I waited a moment and then I added, *I left him.*

The phone rang a second later. Andrew's concerned voice poured into my ear in a stream of frantic syllables. "Where are you, babes? I worried when I didn't see you at Simon's funeral. What did Price do to you? Are you safe? Where are you?"

"It's okay. I'm okay. Calm down."

"What happened?"

God, how to even explain it? I stuck to the simpler facts. "He wouldn't let me go to Simon's funeral. I went ballistic, we got in a huge argument, and he kicked me out."

"He kicked you out?" Andrew sounded incredulous. This was the man who'd clung to me for months with iron control.

"He told me to get the fuck out of his apartment," I said. "But I was ready to go. I couldn't wait to go. I'd reached the point where I'd freaking had enough."

"You have no idea how relieved I am to hear you say that. I've told you before...so many red flags."

"I know."

I didn't tell Andrew about the cage, and the way I'd begged to be let out. I didn't tell him about the fury and terror of being truly powerless, not in a cute, fun, BDSM way but in a real, I'm-trapped-in-an-indestructible-cage kind of way.

"So...I'm at the Gramercy Park Hotel for now," I said. "I didn't want to come there because—"

"Because he'll come here. It's okay. We'll deal with him. Asshole. Why wouldn't he let you go to the funeral? Why is he literally jealous of a guy who's been dead for a week now? Sorry, babes," he said a moment later.

"No, you're right. Simon's dead. I don't know. I was just trying to figure out how I felt about everything. I was hoping for some closure, and when he said I couldn't go, I was kind of like..."

"Kind of like, I fucking hate you?"

"Yeah. Kind of."

"It was an okay funeral," Andrew said. "Although I'm not sure how much closure you would have felt. The guy they were mourning wasn't the guy I knew, the guy who was so shitty to you."

"Were there a lot of people?"

"Tons of people. Mostly art world bigwigs. A few gawkers. Some emo kids and a few reporters. There were a lot of flowers. People got up and talked about Simon's legacy and what he meant to them, and I kept thinking, *what a fucking bunch of bull.* Craig told me to be quiet, because I snorted at one point. So I don't know if being there would have made you feel any better."

My friend was describing exactly what Price had told me would happen. I knew he'd been right, even if I didn't want him to be right. It still didn't excuse incarcerating me so I couldn't go.

"I mean, the funeral was fucked up on so many levels, just like Simon's artwork, and everything in his life," Andrew went on. "All the art farts were carrying on like the Messiah had died. Craig says the value of Simon's work has tripled since last weekend. I guess everyone thought Simon was going to be the next Renoir or Picasso. People were sobbing, Chere. I mean, over *Simon*."

"A lot of people idolized him. You used to idolize him."

"That was before I understood what an ass he was. Chere..." He was silent a moment. "You know his overdose wasn't your fault, right? Nothing Simon ever did was your fault, honey. I know you've had a lot to process the last few days. I imagine it's been a hard week for you."

I laughed at that understatement. "I know it's not my fault, but I can't help feeling bad about everything. And Price... He wouldn't even let me talk about Simon or my feelings. He hated Simon so much. That made things so much harder."

"Well, you know why Price hated Simon. He felt guilty. He couldn't stand that the money he paid you went to Simon. He thought he should have done something about the way Simon abused you."

"He did do something. He eventually got me away from him."

And you kept trying to go back.

I hadn't really gone back, but I'd cried over *Heart-Lust* in Paris, and listened to Simon's pleas when he came to my studio. I'd lost my shit over his death, even though Simon and I hadn't been together in years, even though we never should have been together. I had a weak spot for my ex, a codependent failing. I always had.

I sighed, too softly for Andrew to hear. Price's perspective hit me like a brick to the stomach. He'd bought me a multi-million dollar apartment to get me away from Simon. He'd paid for me to go to design school. He'd left me alone for two years, against his will, so I'd learn to stand on my own two feet. After all that, I'd stubbornly persisted in allowing Simon and his problems back into my life. It must have seemed ungrateful. No, it must have felt like a betrayal.

"None of it matters anymore," I said, shaking my head. I couldn't feel sympathy for Price. He was a bad person, just like Simon was a bad person. Just like I was a bad person sometimes. "I'm through with relationships, and I mean it this time. I'm horrible at them. I truly am. I'm fucking done this time."

"Oh, Chere." It was Andrew's turn to sigh. "Life sucks so bad sometimes. Do you want me to come over? Do you need some cuddle time? Best friend cuddles are the best kind of cuddles."

"They are the best kind of cuddles," I agreed. "But I'm going to take a rain check. I need to take a shower and rest, and think. I need to think about everything. If Price calls you or comes to see you..."

"I won't tell him where you are. He could torture me, and I wouldn't tell him."

"I don't know if he's going to come looking for me," I said, remembering his cold voice. *You have one hour to get the fuck out of this apartment and never come back.* "I might need you to go to his place at some point, though, and get the rest of my things."

"I'll do anything you need me to do. Whatever you need, just call me, any time of day."

"I love you so much, Andrew. You're a wonderful friend."

"The feeling is mutual. You're sure about the cuddles?"

I crawled out of bed and headed toward the bathroom. "Give them to Craig. Appreciate what you have, because he's wonderful." *He doesn't lock you in cages, for instance, to keep you from going to ex-boyfriends' funerals.* "Can you come see me tomorrow? I'll cash in on the cuddles then."

"You got it. You won't even need to get Price's permission first, or confess to him afterward that your gay friend was in the same room with you."

"Freedom. Terrible freedom."

I joked, and Andrew joked, but the freedom really was terrible. Or perhaps it was the loss of security. I'd come to depend on Price for so many things. All of that would have to change. I felt tired just thinking about it, so tired and lost.

I said goodbye to Andrew, unpacked my toiletries and cranked up the shower. I hunched under the hot deluge of water for long minutes, trying to get my muscles to unknot and relax. I washed my hair and every inch of my skin, everywhere Price had ever caressed or struck or groped me. I ate a sandwich from room service that was probably delicious. I didn't know, because I couldn't taste anything.

After that, I turned on the TV to hear some noise, and crawled into the luxurious hotel bed. We'd never watched TV at Price's place. We'd had sex, and played in his dungeon, and when we weren't doing that, we'd read poetry and talked about life and creativity, design and ideas. I didn't allow myself to get up and dig his poetry out of my suitcase. If I did that, I'd never get to sleep.

If I did that, I'd probably run back to him and beg for another chance. That impulse would eventually fade. I just needed distance and time to get over him. He was bad for me. He was just as bad as he'd warned me he was, if only I'd listened.

I hoped I wouldn't dream at all, but I did, stark, suffocating nightmares of pale blue eyes and unbreakable metal bars.

Chapter Fourteen: Barely There

Andrew snuggled beside me, wrapped in the plush hotel comforter. He told the best stories. He was describing the most recent power exchange scene between him and Craig.

"So then he said, 'How much do you love me?' And I was like, 'a whole lot.' And he was like, 'no, I mean, how much do you *love me*?' He wanted me to pick which ass plug he was going to use on me. And Chere, some of them were like..." His voice drifted off as he made exaggerated motions of largeness with his hands. "And he *looked* at me, you know? He just gave me that look, and I loved him so, so much for making me feel so, so fucking scared."

"I know that look," I said, a little sadly. "So? Tell me the rest. Which one did you pick? How much do you love him?"

"Let me put it this way. My ass still hurts, and this was two days ago. I'm lying down instead of sitting. You do the math."

"You got a spanking too, I bet. Bad boy."

"Shit, yeah. Craig likes to make it hurt." He ran a hand through his hair with a giddy smile. Andrew loved getting hurt. Hell, I loved getting hurt too. Fear, dread, the pushing of limits, the emotional appeal.

Do you love me?

Yes, I love you. But I shouldn't. I can't.

Andrew's expression sobered as he looked at his watch. I was expecting Vinod to come by any minute for a brainstorming session. I figured he was coming to check on me too, since I'd been sad when I saw him last week, and had now moved into a hotel. I knew he'd ask questions, and I didn't have the answers, not yet.

"Price texted me a couple more times," Andrew said quietly. "I don't know if you want to know that. I don't know if it matters. I just don't answer them."

I sighed. "Thanks. Sorry if he's bugging you."

"He's not really bugging me. He just keeps asking if you need anything. But I already told him you're fine, so I think he's just looking for excuses to contact me. Maybe he thinks I'll drop some hint about where you're staying."

"If he wanted to find me, he would have done it by now. I mean, my phone is on his plan, and he has other ways of searching for me. Surveillance and investigators. Hunting binoculars. Remember that?"

Andrew shuddered. "How could I forget?"

But he hadn't tried that hard to find me, and he hadn't come by. Every time room service knocked on the door, I thought, maybe... But no. I couldn't say I was hiding anymore, because Price wasn't looking. I was just living in a hotel, waiting to start some new life.

"Thanks for coming to hang out with me," I said. "Next time, I'll schedule us a massage."

There was an obnoxiously loud knock at the door. Andrew's eyes widened.

"It's just Jino," I said. "Vinod's bodyguard. His fists are the size of your head."

"Mmm. Bodyguard fists," Andrew cooed, jumping off the bed. He shrugged into his coat while I went to answer the door. Vinod and Jino bustled in, still cold from outside, wrapped in coats, gloves, and hats. Vinod looked surprised when he noticed Andrew.

"Entertaining handsome young men in your room?" he joked. "You'll make Mr. Eriksen jealous."

"Mr. Eriksen has no right to be jealous," I said.

"Mr. Eriksen has no reason to be jealous," Andrew joked with a swishy tilt of his head.

"Oh." Vinod chuckled. "It's like that."

Andrew was a terminal flirt, and Vinod, that old letch, was giving him the once over right in front of his bodyguard boyfriend Jino. I pictured the two of them double-teaming my friend and got a little turned on by the visual. And a little squicked out. But mostly turned on, maybe because my sex life had gone from two or three encounters a day to zero in the space of a week.

"Vinod, this is my best friend Andrew. Andrew, this is Vinod Sushil and his bodyguard, Jino. Vinod is a trailblazer in Asian ready-to-wear."

Vinod stopped mentally undressing Andrew long enough to turn to me with a smile. "A trailblazer, eh? Flattery will get you everywhere. And what do you do with your life?" he asked, turning back to Andrew.

"I'm a painter."

"A painter?" Vinod stopped leering. His eyes brightened with approval. "I love artists. What do you paint?"

"Anything that moves me," said Andrew with a smile. "I love to make everyday things special and beautiful."

"Ah, then we are in accord, because I also like to make everyday things special and beautiful. What else is life about?" He dug out a card and gave it to Andrew. "Send me a link to some of your work. I love to collect."

He wanted to collect all right—collect Andrew right into his bed. Andrew pocketed the card. "It was very nice to meet you, Mr. Sushil." He nodded to the bodyguard too, who was twice his size. "I'll leave you all to it."

We hugged and he left, his oversized messenger bag banging against his hip. He really was adorable. And taken. "He has a pretty serious boyfriend," I said to Vinod as his eyes lingered on the door.

"So do I," said the old man. "What's your point?"

We both laughed, and then he returned to his usual businesslike self. We sat at the table and started going over some of the tweaks he'd asked for the last time we met together. I showed him the pieces I'd worked up, but most were still in the sketch stage. He touched the paper, trying to visualize.

"This would be dark gold?" he asked, considering a tie pin. "Bronze?"

"I don't know. What do you think?"

"I can't think unless I see it. Unless I feel it in my hands. Show me something else that's similar."

We talked some more, and then he asked how I felt about adding some women's items to the upcoming order. How did I feel about it? I felt fucking ecstatic. The women's market was ten times larger than men's. I'd been waiting all this time for him to ask. But now...

"I don't have that many samples here. There are so many things I want to show you. Can I send you pictures?"

"We can go to your studio right now. Jino will drive us, if you're not too busy." He looked pointedly around the hotel room. "You don't look busy."

"I've been drawing."

"Drawing? I need to see things. I want to hold things in your workshop. Why are you here? Why not in your studio?"

"I'm taking a break from my studio. The thing is..." I knew he'd talk me into going if I didn't tell him everything, confess all the drama. "The thing is, Price and I have broken up, and my studio's in the same building as his office."

Vinod studied me, his lined, bronze face an inscrutable mask.

"So I just feel, you know, too nervous to go there. I don't feel comfortable being so near him. I need to find a new place to work."

"A new place? You have a studio on Park Avenue, in a magnificent building. Where else will you go?"

"I don't know." I pressed my hands together, feeling defensive. Jino watched us with his large, dark eyes.

"My dear, are you so terribly afraid of running into him?" Vinod said. "What did he do to you, to make you feel this way?"

"He didn't do anything," I lied. "I just don't want there to be a confrontation. An argument or something." *He might touch me then. He might try to win me back.*

And I might go back to him.

I spread my hands in apologetic finality. "I just can't. I won't feel safe there."

Vinod tsked. "It's your studio, yes? You have a right to work in your own place." He gestured toward his hulking sidekick. "Jino can go with us. He can protect you from any confrontations. He's very good at keeping people in line."

I tried not to notice the salacious look my elderly mentor exchanged with his much younger bodyguard before he turned back to me.

"Jino won't let anyone interfere with you if you don't wish it. I promise, you'll be safe as can be. Look at him. He loves beating people up if he gets the chance."

Jino nodded and tapped his fists together. I rolled my eyes.

"I don't want Jino to beat up Price." The image didn't please me. I didn't feel spiteful toward Price, I just felt numb. And confused. And lonely all the fucking time.

"Can you give me one more week to get some samples together for you? Please?" I asked Vinod. "I'm going to handle everything and get back in the studio. I just need a little more time."

"I can give you two weeks," said Vinod. "A month, you know, whatever. I can give you as long as your inspiration needs. But I am worried about you, my dear. An artist must be in the studio, submerging herself in her art. You cannot only be here in this empty room, drawing up plans."

"I know."

He took my hand and squeezed it. "My buyers love your work. I see it now in the advertisements, on billboards. On people. You are successful, but you are not happy. This upsets me. Does it upset you, Jino?"

His stone-faced companion responded with an almost half-nod. For Jino, it was enthusiastic agreement. Vinod looked at me as if to say, *See?*

"Happiness takes time," I muttered. "Happiness is something you have to work at."

"No," he said, drawing himself up in his impeccably tailored suit. "Happiness lives inside you. Where is your happiness?"

He asked in such a demanding tone that I thought I should answer, but I didn't understand the question. Did he mean where in my life? Where in my mind? Where, geographically? My mind darted like a reckless kid in front of a car, straight to Bleecker Street.

"I don't think I've ever been happy," I said peevishly. "It's not that easy for everyone. I'm happy if you're happy—"

"And I'm unhappy that you're unhappy," he snapped back in his crotchety-old-retail-magnate tone. "You make beautiful things, Chere. If you were happier, think how much more beautiful they might be."

"Sometimes you annoy me," I said, closing my sketchbook.

"I assure you that you annoy me much more. Isn't that right, Jino?"

This time Jino gave a full nod. Traitor.

Vinod sighed and began to gather up his things. "I'll give you the time you need to find more happiness, Chere. I'm going back to India for a while, at least for the next few weeks. That is where I am happiest." He gave me a very sharp, direct look. "And so, you see, that is where I always return."

* * * * *

I leaned back in my chair and rubbed the muscles at the base of my neck. I was supposed to be finishing a bridge design for the City of Vancouver. Instead I had two computer windows open, one to Chere's studio camera feed, and the other to the guest room feed at our apartment.

Not that I would have gone after her if I saw her. I just wanted to be sure she was okay. She'd been gone a week now, and I didn't know where the fuck she was, which kept me in a constant state of uneasiness. She hadn't gone to Andrew's. I'd called him, and he said she wasn't there, but that she'd gone someplace safe. He said I had to leave her alone, and I agreed, or I would have put a tail on him by now to find out where she was holed up. I was sure Andrew had visited her at some point. That little shit didn't respond to any of my other texts pleading for information.

Does she need anything? Is she okay?

Of course she was okay. She was away from me, wasn't she?

"Price?"

Jennifer said my name again, a little louder. "Price? Did you hear David's question?"

I tore my gaze from the camera feeds. "What? No, I'm sorry."

"About the proportion of the towers and suspender cables?" said David. "I don't question the viability of the structure, but the design is so...spare."

"I want it to be spare. It's the Un-bridge. That's the whole point."

We'd been over this already. Vancouver wanted a bridge, and I wanted to try something new, an homage to Chere's spare and delicate jewelry designs, only scaled to massive size.

"I've done the math," I said. David, the fucking upstart. "Praneesh has looked at it too. The numbers work."

"I'm sure the math works, but you'll have to light the towers and the main cables. Otherwise, no one will see them."

"I don't care. It doesn't matter. Bridges don't have to be solid, inflexible behemoths. This one can move with the earth."

Jennifer and Hannah were on David's side, even though the City of Vancouver was on board with the visionary design.

"They want something new," said Praneesh. "Vancouver's a progressive city."

"It's barely there," David persisted. "People won't feel secure when they're on it. It's not appropriate bridge design."

"Not appropriate?" I wanted to follow that up by shouting "Fuck you and what's appropriate," but I kept the words inside, because this was a business meeting and I was the boss, and I had to present a composed and capable front. That way, when my associates told me something wasn't appropriate, that a design wouldn't work, I could stand my ground and say, yes, it fucking will.

Because there was always a way to make things work, if you looked hard enough. I'd done the math and calculated countless distances and angles. I'd designed the safest, most understated, environmentally friendly, weatherproof, and elegant bridge anyone had ever seen, and fuck me if some MIT grad with a hard-on for girders and concrete was going to tell me it *wasn't appropriate.*

"The cost of the lights will be offset by the durability of the materials," I said. "If you start adding more bulk to the cables and towers merely for visibility—"

"Visibility is an important part of bridge design."

"So is innovation," I snapped.

"It's just..." Hannah the peacemaker spoke up. "It's just a real departure from our usual designs. I think it's beautiful and viable, just...really different."

"It's growth. It's expanding our portfolio. It's changing with the times, moving from amplification and ostentation to refined simplicity. In that setting, in that geographical location, it will work."

The voices at the table went quiet as I showed them the renderings again. This wasn't just about the bridge; it was about the bridge's place in the world. Funny how it had taken Chere's unconventional aesthetic to teach me that.

God, Chere. It still fucking hurt to think about her. I stared back at the camera feeds while my associates debated the merits and drawbacks of the Vancouver bridge. Through the haze of my disaffected pain, I could hear David and Hannah coming around and admitting it was a visionary project. That should have made me happy, but it was an empty victory. The woman who had inspired this elegant vision was gone.

We put the Vancouver plans aside and moved on to other projects on the docket. Chere was gone, but life went on. Cities expanded, skylines changed, and structures came into existence through deep and thoughtful planning. There was more work to do. There would always be work to do, even if there was no one to share it with in my personal life.

Jesus, I was so fucking lonely without her. I still loved her, that was the fucked up thing. I'd always love her, just as she'd always loved Simon, even though their whole thing was a train wreck. Sometimes there were just *bonds* between people. Not manacles or leather cuffs or rope, but bonds deep inside you, because someone understood you and accepted you despite all your pathetic flaws.

But whatever. I could still work. I could go home and eat, and read, and drink wine now and again to remind me there was some good in life, even if I didn't have Chere kneeling at my feet. I was on my second glass of wine Thursday night, deep in the poems of Percy Shelley, when my phone pinged with a text from Vinod. Because of his association with Chere, we'd become something more than business acquaintances.

I'm leaving for India soon, he wrote. *Need anything?*

I thought a moment, then texted, *Saffron from Kashmir. And Kismi Bars. Hundreds of them.*

He texted a line of pig emojis, then the words *As you wish.*

I frowned at the screen, wondering if Vinod had been in contact with Chere since she left me. They used to speak by phone at least once a week. I could ask him if he'd been in contact with her, but it was none of my business, since Chere and I weren't together anymore.

Safe travels, I typed instead, hoping to draw the conversation to a close before I said something I shouldn't.

All is well with you? he texted. *And Chere?*

I didn't know what to reply. Nothing was well with me these days. Work was a hassle, home was an awful, empty place, and strangers were living in Chere's apartment. *Everything's fine*, I typed, just to give an answer.

Is it? I only wonder why you're letting someone so dear to you live in a hotel. A nice hotel, the Gramercy, but still.

I stared down at the message. The Gramercy. The place I'd left her.

You saw her there? I texted.

Just today.

A pause, and then another text popped up on my screen.

Why is she there, I wonder? He inserted a few goggle-eyed emojis. *None of my business. I'll bring you saffron and chocolate.*

I typed two words in response. *Thank you.*

I wasn't thanking him for saffron and chocolate. I was thanking him because I finally knew where she was.

Fuck.

I finally knew where she was.

CHAPTER FIFTEEN:
ALL THE WRONG, BAD THINGS

I was lingering over coffee, staring out the window on Saturday morning, when a loud, pounding knock jolted me from my thoughts. I didn't mind, because they were shitty thoughts, unfocused and conflicted even after a week of cowardly huddling in this room.

I knew Vinod was supposed to leave for India today, which was probably why Jino was pounding on my door at this hour. I threw the lock and opened it, expecting to find my silver-haired friend and his towering sidekick. I remembered too late that Price also had an aggressive knock, one he wasn't afraid to use in the quiet hallways of luxury hotels.

My ex-Master looked beautiful and tired, his jaw scruffy with a day's worth of stubble. He wore a gray coat with an ivory sweater, and flawlessly pressed pants that highlighted his muscular physique. His gaze was as blue and deep as it had ever been. A bundle of white tulips peeked from beneath his arm.

I stared at him, not ready for this moment. "How did you know where—"

"Vinod."

He didn't make a move to come in. I studied his expression as I had so many times, trying to decipher what he felt. As usual, he gave me nothing. Irritation washed over me. I focused it on the tulips. I'd always hated tulips.

"Flowers aren't going to fix us," I said.

"I know. These aren't for you, they're for Simon." He finally reached toward me, but didn't quite touch me. "I'm taking you to the cemetery. Do you need a coat?"

"The cemetery? Why?"

"So you can have your fucking closure."

I frowned at him in exasperation. "This is all a little too late, don't you think?"

I finally saw something in his face, some human emotion. Panic. "Will you please just come?" He reached out again, and this time he took my hand. "Please come with me, Chere. We need to talk."

I sighed and went for a coat. Price stood at the door, looking around the hotel room. Wondering where to install the cameras? Or was he remembering the last time he'd come here, to leave that note that destroyed my life?

And then rebuilt your life, Chere. Don't forget that.

Simon's final resting place was in Fair Lawn, a half hour outside the city. Price had said we needed to talk, but we rode in the back of his chauffeured sedan in total silence most of the way. Price was in scary self-control mode. He wouldn't even look at me. The tulips trembled on his lap, their delicate white petals too blatant in design for my tastes. I liked the mystery of roses, the frivolity of carnations.

Flowers for Simon. Did he think that would win me back?

But I'd missed Simon's funeral, and I hadn't had the heart to visit his grave on my own, so I might as well visit it with Price, even if everything felt weird. Maybe this was his idea of closure, but closure for whom? For him, for his guilt in making me miss Simon's funeral? Even if it was for me, this trip to the cemetery was only necessary because of what *he'd* done.

"It has to be on your terms, doesn't it?"

I didn't realize I'd spoken aloud until Price looked over at me. "What? What has to be on my terms?"

"Simon. His death. This final goodbye, or whatever you have planned."

He was silent a moment, then he shrugged. "You're probably right."

"Forget it, then. I want to go back to the hotel."

"We're not going back. We're going to Simon's fucking grave and we're going to put these fucking flowers on it."

I let out a huff and pressed back against the seat, and stared out the window. "Tulips are my least favorite flower."

"I don't care."

Ah, how I'd missed his bright, sunny personality. I wished I was on a plane to India instead. Vinod had invited me to go with him, but I'd refused because it seemed too far to go when my life was a mess.

You didn't go because you would have been too far away from Price.

Ugh, I hated that I still loved him. I hated that I was fighting off tears because he was so close to me, holding those ugly, floppy flowers in his lap. I hated that I'd been waiting for him to come for me, even while I hid and told myself I was gathering strength to move on. I had no strength. I was an idiot, and always had been.

When we got to the cemetery, I jumped out before he could come around and open my door. I scanned the expanse of lawn and weathered memorials. It was easy to find Simon's grave. There was no headstone yet, but there were piles of flowers and beribboned reproductions of his work. A couple art school kids hovered nearby, poking through the bouquets and cards. Price's scowl sent them scurrying back to their car.

Once they left, he turned to me, holding out the tulips. I didn't take them. I couldn't take them. I was too preoccupied with the dirt. All the flowers and notes people had left didn't cover the bare rectangle of turned earth packed down over Simon's remains. The man who'd pleaded with me at my studio mere days ago was under that dirt now, in the ground, forever. *Shit. Don't cry. Don't fucking cry.*

Price leaned down and put the tulips near the other piles of potted plants and bouquets. I wondered if Simon's family came here every day to look at them. His parents had moved here from Florida years ago to try to help him. I wondered if they could bear to visit with all that dirt staring them in the face. Why couldn't I help him? Even before Price's interference, I couldn't help. For years and years, I couldn't help.

For years and years, I'd known it would end this way.

Still, I said, "I can't believe he's dead," like an idiot. It was more that I couldn't believe he was *under that dirt*, buried in some box. He was dead, and he wasn't coming back, and that was why I finally started bawling, because there was *I guess this is the end of us* and then there was fucking death.

Price came to stand beside me, a pillar to steady me as I wept. "You must be happy," I said bitterly between sobs. "Your rival is gone."

"Why does it matter?"

He didn't say it in a mean way, the way I'd sounded. He said it like he was stating a fact. Yes, why did it matter? Price was out of my life the same way Simon was out of my life, with one big difference. Price wasn't dead, buried under six feet of dirt in a quiet New Jersey cemetery. The idea of Price and death made me clutch at him like he needed saving, like the earth might open up and take him too.

He brushed away my tears as I clung to his elbows, like I had any power to rescue either one of us.

"Just tell me you understand that this isn't your fault," he said gruffly, as more tears replaced the ones he wiped away. "That's the reason I was so stubborn about all this. About his funeral. I should have let you go to the damn thing, but I..." He made a vicious face, staring down at the flowers, all colors, all kinds. "I was right about not letting you help Simon, because he was beyond saving. He would have turned you inside out again, and he'd already hurt you enough. But I was wrong about the funeral. After all those years, everything you suffered, you earned the right to say goodbye."

"It's a little late to realize that now."

"I know. When it comes to you, I always figure things out too late."

"What does that mean?"

He shook his head, wisely refusing to talk about us. It was too dangerous at the moment, with him apologizing and me in tears. We looked down at the grave instead, and I realized I really had nothing left to say to Simon Baldwin or the dirt that covered him. I'd said goodbye years ago, whether Price believed me or not. As for my guilt in the saga of Simon's terrible choices, I'd have to find a way to let that go.

I turned back toward the car, drawing our visit to a close. *Goodbye, Simon. Goodbye, Chere's fucked-up past life.* It was time to move on.

Price opened the door and I slid across the seat, mopping at my eyes. They stung from crying, and I had a headache. I used to deal with pain and discomfort all the time at Price's hands. I loved that kind of pain, but the pain I brought on myself was unbearable.

He climbed in beside me and shut the door. "Are you okay?" he asked. "Do you want to get something to eat?" He studied me in consternation. "You look like you've lost weight."

"I'm fine," I said too quickly. I wasn't fine at all. I was lying to him again. Dishonesty. Jealousy. Lack of trust. Those were the things that had doomed our relationship from the start.

"No," I said instead. "I'm not okay. I haven't been eating, or sleeping. I'm barely surviving without you. Even now..." I couldn't admit all the specifics. I couldn't say how magnificent he seemed to me with his stern, tightly controlled emotions, or how drawn I felt to the pain he held inside. "Even now, I still have feelings for you."

"Then why are you at the Gramercy?" A glimmer of raw vulnerability flashed in his eyes. "Why aren't you with me?"

"Because you're an asshole. Because you wouldn't let me safeword out of your cage."

"I wouldn't let you out because you wouldn't listen to me. You wouldn't trust me. You've never trusted me."

"You've never proven yourself worthy of my trust!"

My voice sounded loud in the sedan. The driver remained stone-faced, pretending not to hear our tortured conversation. I wished I didn't have to hear it. My emotional nerve endings felt scraped raw.

"Chere," he said, reaching to stroke my face. Damn, I was crying again. My eyes were killing me. He was killing me.

"Don't," I said, pushing his hand away. "Just don't."

"Everything I've done to you, all the wrong, bad things..." he murmured sorrowfully. "It was all because I love you. I told you, I don't know how to love the right way."

"Then I guess there's no hope for us." My voice sounded bitchy, but my soul was bleeding. "I can't survive like this. My heart can't take this anymore."

"Mine can't either. Something has to change."

We rode in silence for a few minutes with those words between us. *Something has to change.* But what could we change? He couldn't turn sweet and genteel. I needed his rough edges, and he wouldn't be able to pull off the genteel thing anyway. I wanted him to be who he was, and I wanted to be who I was, a surrendered submissive who still needed to fight every now and then.

Were we impossible? Were we hopeless?

"I miss you so much," I said. "But I don't know how to live with you."

"I don't know how to live with you, either. I don't know how to find that line between having you and letting you go. Not letting you go from my life, but letting you go enough to let you live your life." He rubbed his eyes and growled in frustration. "I'm too afraid of losing you. I've been looking... Fuck. I've been looking so long for love, for acceptance. My parents were absent, my nannies hated me because I was a shit. My grandmother...she died when I was young. The women I dated loved my money, my body, but none of them loved me. None of them accepted me. Only you. And I feel like if I don't..." His hands clenched in his lap. "I worry if I don't hold you tightly enough..."

I stared at his whitening knuckles, searching the spaces between his words to find some way to fix us.

"You don't have to lock me away to make me love you," I said. "Don't you understand that? I loved you before. Your passion, your poetry, all of it changed me. God, I've loved you for so long."

"You loved me until I put you in my dungeon."

I placed a hand over his. "Even then, I loved you. You were the one who fell apart. You were the one who wouldn't trust me, who came up with all these controlling rules that were more about suspicion and jealousy than keeping me safe."

He made another frustrated sound. "I thought you liked control and rules."

"I do. I love them, but I wish they came from a place of love rather than fear." I studied his profile, his strong, thoughtful brow. "You're right," I said softly. "Something has to change. But it's not you, or me. It's this constant fear we live with, this fear that our relationship's going to end."

"But we did end," he said. "Many times."

"Because we're fuck ups. Because we're afraid of everything that might go wrong."

He gave me a sideways look. "I hate being afraid."

"I hate it too. It's exhausting. We need to fucking change."

The car stopped at a light. People bustled through the crosswalk, lugging Saturday shopping bags and shouldering for space. The city was busy, always busy, but inside the car, time seemed suspended. Change was scary, but living without one another was so much scarier. I prayed he was brave enough to change for me, to at least try. I was brave enough. The fighter inside me was stirring to life.

"Can you change?" I prompted. "Can you let the fears go? I know I'll have to do it, too. But I will, for you."

He didn't answer. He stared instead at my hand over his. *Take my hand. Hold my hand. Please, try, for us.*

He stirred suddenly, like he was coming out of a trance, then looked at me with his brows drawn together. "For a couple months now, I've been designing this bridge. It's not like anything I've done before. It's simple and spare, because of you. Because you showed me that that could be beautiful." His eyes burned me with their intensity. "I didn't think there'd be a way to do it, but I figured it out and showed it to everyone. No one liked it at first, but I kept trying to make them see. I kept trying. I made it work."

I swallowed past the emotion in my throat. "And did they see?"

"Yes. I told you, there's always a way."

I held up a finger. "No, *I* told you there was always a way. Remember? I put that sign in my window."

"I remember," he said.

"Because you were fucking up again."

"I'm pretty sure you were fucking up too."

He finally laced his fingers through mine, and brought my hand to his lips. They felt warm and firm. How many times had I kissed those lips?

"I know we can work," he said. "There's always a way. There has to be a way for us, because it's important. I'll change the way I act, to make things better. I'll adjust."

His words unsettled me. I knew we needed to work together to fix things, but I didn't want the essence of Price to go away. I needed his commanding personality, his dominance and requirements. "I don't want you to change too much," I said. "I still want you to be you."

"I'll still be me, but you need to tell me what *you* need. You're part of this too."

"You know what I need. You've always known."

"Jesus," he said, running a hand through his hair. "There's nothing more frustrating than trying to communicate with a submissive."

"But you *know*," I argued. "You know the good parts of our relationship, and the parts that didn't work. I want the things that were good. The passion. The sex and drama. The dungeon, and the kisses afterward in your arms. The poetry."

"The poetry." He made an impatient gesture. "It's not enough, for all you do for me."

"You're enough for me, just as you are. Well, slightly changed. Minus the fears and jealousy."

He shook his head and gave a rough laugh. "I can't believe I'm enough for you."

"Believe it."

"My poems don't even rhyme."

"Poems don't have to rhyme to be beautiful."

Look at what you do for me, I thought. *You're so beautiful.*

He let out a slow breath. "You know, I only ever wrote poems for you. You're the only one."

"I know."

He was so fucked up, this freakishly handsome, lonely, neglected, rich boy who'd never known love. All his grand bridges and skyscrapers weren't enough to make him feel worthy of one ghetto-bred ex-hooker.

"I love your poems," I said, "but I don't want the taunt of you anymore. The mystery. The distance. I want *you*, Price. Let me in. I'll be your slave forever, but I need you to be with me too. Do you know what I mean?" I let go of his hand and spread my fingers against his chest. "Be with me. Give me your heart, all of it, without fear and suspicion. I won't hurt you. I won't leave you." I grabbed his face and made him look at me. "I love you."

He gazed into my eyes and put his hands over mine. "You left me," he said.

"You left me too, damn it. But we're going to change. We're not going to leave each other anymore. We're going to find a fucking way."

He stared at me as he squeezed my fingers. "Does that mean you're coming back to me?"

That was the big question, but it was hardly a question. I was almost sitting in his lap. "Do you want me back?" I asked. "You told me to get out of your fucking life."

"I was a little upset when I said that. If I ever say that again, just ignore me because I don't mean it. You belong with me." He let go of my hands to grab my neck. "Come back to me, starshine. When you're ready, I want you to come back. We'll fix everything. We'll make everything better."

He put his thumb against my pulse, and I felt it in the beat of my heart.

CHAPTER SIXTEEN: BEAUTIFUL

There were tons of people in the Gramercy Park lobby when Chere and I returned, and more people in the elevator. I wanted all of them gone. Coming back to this hotel —to *that* room—was difficult enough for me. I'd made so many mistakes. But white tulips were a symbol of forgiveness and new beginnings, and Chere was letting me come upstairs.

I stared at her stubborn little chin in the elevator, and her lovely, elegant neck, so perfect to choke or caress. I loved her. I needed her, and she'd agreed to give our relationship another chance. Something had to change, and it would. I'd figure out what I needed to do to make her happy, and come as close as I could to that. *Poems don't have to rhyme to be beautiful*, she'd said. And love didn't have to be perfect.

You just had to find a way to make it work.

I followed her down the hall to the room. I wasn't sure what she wanted. I wasn't sure if she was ready to come home yet, or if she wanted to talk some more, or if she wanted to fuck. I felt stripped naked from our conversation in the car, and now I was terrified of doing something wrong and causing her to lose hope in us after all.

When she stopped outside the door, I stopped too, and waited. We were like two teenagers after a first date, unsure whether it was okay to kiss. "I haven't kissed you yet," I said. "I want to kiss you."

"You can do that. But first we should go inside."

She flipped her key over in her palm, then slid it into the door. The lock clicked and she went in, but I stayed where I was. "If you let me in..."

"I know."

"I'll do terrible things to you. Rough, uncontrolled things."

"That's kind of what I was hoping."

She stood back and let me through the door, and shut it behind us. We were alone together for the first time in over a week, and I wanted everything, every violent and carnal thing.

No. Wait. I forced myself to be still. I didn't want to take her in a frenzy, so it was over before we realized what was happening. I wanted this reunion to be slow and deliberate, so it would last. I wanted to remember everything, and also rediscover everything. My fingers trembled at the waist of her skirt. I wondered if she had panties on, or if she was still following my rules. I jammed my hand down beneath the material and discovered warm, bare skin.

Good girl, I thought, but the word that came out of my mouth was "Mine."

"Yes," she whispered, leaning into me. "I've been yours for years now."

I slipped my hands under her sweater and traced over her ribs and spine. I flicked open her bra, and then I pulled everything off because I needed her naked. So much for going slow. I tugged down her skirt and she kicked it off, along with her shoes. I looked at her for a second, and then I was on her, biting, devouring, kissing every beautiful curve. She pulled at my coat and sweater, and I yanked them off so we could be skin to skin.

"It's okay to hurt me," she whispered as I twisted fingers in her hair. "I still want you to hurt me."

She wanted recapture. She wanted to submit and kneel before me. I would have given anything for a handful of zip ties. Instead I used my belt to circle her wrists behind her back, and then held her against me to fasten the buckle at the front of her waist. She struggled to free her arms just as she had the first day. Just as she probably always would, which was okay, because it made me want her that much more.

I threw her onto the bed and stripped off my pants, leaving them in a heap on the floor. My cock was hard as fuck. I couldn't wait to get inside her and make her hurt the way she wanted. When she tried to turn to me, I flipped her back over and knelt between her legs. It was so tempting to try to get into her ass, but I didn't have lube, or even a condom to ease the way.

Soon. Later. Maybe tonight.

For now, I pulled her hips up and forced her thighs open. She moaned and buried her head in the sheets, then arched up again as I landed a few sharp slaps on her ass.

"Are you ready? Do you want me?"

"Yes, Sir, please!"

I squeezed her breasts and shoved my aching cock into her pussy. She shuddered as I drove deep, making her mine again. Jesus fuck, the sensation. The tightness. After all the longing and loneliness, it felt almost too good to be inside her. *Go slow. Appreciate all the sexy, wonderful things about her.*

It had been so long since we'd simply fucked, without cages or manacles or all the other shit I kept in the dungeon. Her body was just as beautiful on a bed as it was on a rack or a spanking bench. I yanked her hair hard so I could feel the tension in her pussy. After that, my fingertips searched for her nipples, because when I pinched and twisted them, she always reacted with her hips.

"Hurt me," she begged.

I growled and fucked her deeper, and slapped her ass hard enough to leave a bright red hand print. Soon there was a whole lattice of them, as I delivered noisy blows to the symphony of her cries. We might change in some ways during the days and months ahead, but this would always stay the same. She'd always have marks on her ass, because pain made her hotter and wetter than anything else I could do. Her juices were drowning my dick.

"You want to be hurt?" I asked.

Fuck. *Fuck.* Sometimes only one kind of hurt would do. I was going to take her ass after all, with some spit and pussy juice, because she needed it, and I wanted it.

"I'm going to stick it in your ass," I said roughly. "Don't fucking try to stop me."

She made a sound that wasn't yes or no, just the sound of someone being fucked so hard and so deep that she was pretty much up for anything. I pulled out and made her turn so she was on her back, and then shoved her legs up over my shoulders. She met my gaze with gorgeous dread as I spread her pussy lips and fingerfucked the hell out of her.

"You're so fucking wet," I said, shoving the moisture down toward her hole. "But I think it's still going to hurt you."

She squirmed then, until I clapped my hands over her thighs to still her. I lubed up my cock with more pussy juice and then spit on her asshole to turn her on.

"Please go slow," she said as I probed her tiny hole with my dick.

"Please shut the fuck up. You said you wanted to be hurt."

"Since when do you do what I say?" she sassed.

I put my hand over her mouth. "No more words. Pretend we're in the dungeon. No talking."

That got her hotter still. She loved when I took her speech away. Someday I'd do the eye contact thing too, and not allow her to look at me. It would be like the first day, with the mask, only this would be hotter, because she wouldn't be terrified for her life the way she'd been at the W Hotel.

But I wanted her eye contact today. She looked wonderfully scared and horny, with her arms bound and her legs spread. I pressed into her ass, using her own moisture as lube. It wasn't really enough to make things easy, but it was enough to get in. Her breath came in sharp, frantic pants as I stretched her asshole open. Oh, I was being very slow and deliberate now.

I held her gaze as I eased my way in, insisting that she open her eyes whenever she tried to close them from the pain. That was why I'd turned her over, so I could see the agony and ecstasy in real time, and of course, so I didn't really hurt her any more than she wanted to be hurt. I was halfway in, and she was still struggling against me. I leaned on one hand and wrapped the other around her neck.

"Let go," I said. "Let me do what I want." I released her for a moment to slap her, then I grabbed her neck harder, digging my fingers into her skin. I could see the tumble into subspace, the helpless

166

submission to my force and will. She made a sobbing sound in her throat, and she wasn't asking me to stop. She was asking me to go harder.

I smiled. I couldn't help it. "You don't know a thing about self-preservation. Now give up your fucking asshole. This isn't over until I get what I want."

My fingers tightened on her windpipe. Her cheek was pink where I'd slapped it.

"Look at me," I ordered when she started to go woozy. I let her breathe a little as I eased the rest of the way into her ass. She arched and pushed against my cock, and I had to steel myself not to go off right then. It felt delicious, this conquering. Her surrender. One required the other, which was why I'd treasure her forever. I stared down at my cock buried in her spasming hole. Wetness still seeped down her crack, because, by some miracle, this turned her on.

"I bet this feels awful," I taunted her. "I bet it feels scary and dangerous."

She moaned in response, and opened her mouth even though no words came out. I massaged her neck and she lengthened it, as if inviting me to have her breath if I wanted it. Fuck me, I wanted it. I gave her a hard, forceful, riotous kiss as I started to move in her ass. Now that the entry was accomplished, there were plenty of slippery juices to keep us going. Her moans drove me mad.

"Look at me," I said. "Don't take your eyes off me."

I slapped her a couple more times to get my point across, then I kissed her again. She pressed her hips toward mine, shuddering every time I bottomed out inside her. Her non-verbal exclamations fell somewhere between *ow* and *yes*, which summed up the magic of our relationship, and the reason we needed to be together.

"You're mine." I stared into her depthless brown eyes and made her believe it. "You'll always be mine, in this. In everything."

Oh, God. She was using her bound hands to pull apart her ass cheeks, to offer me that much more of herself. *And she is Lust... Mine also, little painted poem of God.*

I rewarded this groveling submission with more fingers on her windpipe. This time, I didn't stop to give her breath. She knew by now when I was putting her out. She usually resisted or at least made some small, pleading sound, but this time she held my gaze in utter trust, in fearless, abject surrender. I didn't want her to go. I wanted to hold that yielding gaze and save that moment forever, but physiology worked by certain rules, and a moment later, her body went slack, her eyes closed, and she was gone.

Now I was the one shuddering as I surged inside her. In those fleeting moments before she came to, she was vulnerable, helpless, and entirely mine. Even when she returned to consciousness, her body remained open to me.

"You're back," I said, stroking a thumb across her cheek.

Her hazy eyes focused on mine. A moment later, she seemed to remember where she was. She became aware that her hands were still bound, and that she still had a cock buried firmly in her ass.

"Hurt me," she whispered.

I let the forbidden speech slide, because I liked what she was saying, and because she still wasn't quite awake. I also did as she requested, torturing her nipples some more as I held off my orgasm, and giving her a few more resounding spanks. Each slap of pain, each excruciating twist and pinch wound her up more. When she was wild with distress and lust, I drove deep inside her ass and held there.

"I want you to come when I tell you," I said. "I want to feel you gripping my dick, and I want to hear how good it feels for you. Not yet. Wait for me. When I say."

I fondled her sex, caressing her clit, tracing over it with all her juices. She was gone in a wonderful way, thrusting and straining at my belt, arching her hips for a harder, deeper invasion.

"Not yet," I said. "I know you want to come, but you obey me."

She tried to twist away from my teasing caresses, making frantic noises in her throat.

"Oh, I bet you're close. Just a moment longer."

When I thought she might literally expire, I palmed her clit, charmed by the way she bucked up against me. "Come now," I said. "Remember, I want to feel it. I want to hear it."

She threw her head back and cried out, kicking her legs through a trembling orgasm. I'd wound her up for my own amusement, but I'd become pretty wound up too, so that when she squeezed around me, the pleasure almost hurt me. I gritted my teeth, not just from the strength of my orgasm, but the fact that I'd reduced her to base animal lust, and she'd surrendered enough to let me do it.

"Fuck," she said. "Oh, fuck." She opened her eyes and looked at me, half there and half gone. "May I talk again?"

"Did I say you could talk again?"

She grimaced and squirmed some more, and I kissed her until my dick went soft and she went soft too. Only then did I undo the belt and release her arms. The first thing she did was throw them around my neck.

"Can I talk now?" she asked.

"I wish I had the gag," I teased. "Your favorite cock gag." I decided I'd improvise one later, using my own cock. "But yes, okay, starshine. I guess you can talk."

"I just wanted to say that I love you." Her lips brushed against my ear. "I missed you. I even missed getting fucked in the ass by you."

"Because you love getting fucked in the ass," I said, holding her close.

"I love your roughness. I don't want that to change."

I chuckled at her anxious expression. "Based on what just happened, I think we'll be okay. And you should know that I have a lot of rough and dirty impulses built up inside me. It's been a week since I've had you."

She started to sit up. "A week's not that long."

I shoved her back down against the bedsheets. "You know what's going to be long? Today. This afternoon. Tonight. Tomorrow. I'm just getting started with you."

She looked a little nervous, but she mostly looked happy.

"A shower and some room service?" I suggested. "You're going to need your strength."

* * * * *

I woke to a slash of sunlight streaming through the dark velvet curtains, and Price's heavy form strewn across my back. I turned my head to look at the clock. Late morning already. I'd slept like the dead, which made sense, since Price had pretty much killed me with our sexual reunion. Memories flooded back, all the fucking and grappling of the night before.

I groaned and tried to extricate myself from his embrace. He grumbled but let me go. He'd stayed up even later than me, stroking my back and my hair, whispering to me as I drifted off to sleep. *Mine.* That was the gist of what he'd told me, over and over. *You're mine.* As for me, I'd told him what he needed to hear to soothe his secret, crippling anxieties. *I love you. I need you. You're perfect, and I adore you just as you are.*

I stumbled into the bathroom and dialed the lights down low, and started the shower. I was halfway through brushing my teeth before I looked up and saw the writing on the mirror. Not just writing, but art too, hearts and jewels and a cityscape, and remarkably good likenesses of me and Price. I looked closer at the scarlet and pink lines, and realized he'd done the whole thing in my lipstick. There were three empty tubes on the counter. A poem took up most of the mirror, written in his now-familiar hand.

What you see right now
Is what I see when I dream.
Beautiful diamond, beautiful heart.
Beautiful fighter, and a soul like art.

I was so gripped by his poem, so spellbound by the depth of feeling in those scrawls of lipstick, that I didn't hear him come into the bathroom. I jumped when he hugged me from behind.

"I'm no world class artist," he said. "And it still doesn't fucking rhyme, but I hope you like it."

I turned and threw my arms around him. "It kind of rhymes. I love it. It's... Holy crap. I love you." I clung to his neck and breathed him in as he groped my ass. "You wrote 'beautiful' three times."

"Because you're beautiful in so many ways. You're everything in that poem, and so much more."

His caresses were wonderful, but still not as thrilling as the affection in his voice. "When did you do this?" I asked, letting go of him.

"Last night, while you were sleeping." He glanced at the empty tubes on the counter. "Sorry about your lipstick. I'll replace them."

"Forget the lipstick." I turned back to his artwork as tears gathered in my eyes. "It's so lovely, Price. It's my favorite poem ever."

"Don't cry." He frowned at me in the mirror, over my shoulder. "It's not supposed to make you cry. It's supposed to make you happy."

"It does make me happy." I cried anyway, just a few tears, while he rolled his eyes and brushed his teeth.

"So what now?" he said after he spit. "Do you want to ease back into things?"

I stretched my sore muscles. "Was last night 'easing back into things'?"

"Last night was hot sex," he said with a grin. "I mean the rest of our life together. The surrender. The slavery."

"Yes, I still want that, if you want it."

"Do I want it? Let me think about that a moment." He slapped me on the ass. Hard. "Yes. But no more sex until I go back to the apartment and collect a few things."

"You don't want me to go too?"

"Not yet. Don't worry, I'll be back," he assured me when my face fell. His fingertips traced along the worry lines in my brow. "I don't want to hole up in the apartment with you yet. I think we should spend a little more time on neutral ground. The dungeon will still be there, I promise." He gave me a mocking smile. "Naughty girl."

"Naughty girls need dungeons," I grumbled as he went out into the other room to dress.

"I'll bring back some things for your amusement," he promised. "And mine."

The last two words were accompanied by a wonderfully threatening leer.

I sprawled on the bed and watched him dress, pants and clinging undershirt and sweater. God, the muscles. It was still hard to believe sometimes that this powerful, complicated man belonged to me.

"Do you think you would have been able to find me if Vinod hadn't helped you?" I asked.

"Eventually. I would have come for you when my willpower ran out, just like last time." He fastened his belt, then jammed a hand in his pocket. "Speaking of which..." He returned to the bed with something between his fingers. "I suppose you better put this back on." He held out the garnet ring I'd left with Andrew. His lips tilted down as he slid it on my finger. "You can wear it for now, until I get something better. Something more permanent."

He put it on my left ring finger, my engagement finger, with a deeply speaking gaze. Wow. Yes. My answer would be yes, of course, when he asked, although I didn't really need anything better or more permanent.

His rough, pure, achingly sincere love would always be enough.

CHAPTER SEVENTEEN: POETRY AND LOVE

Price and I stayed at the Gramercy for almost a month. It was an extravagance, sure, but also necessary. As Price pointed out, the hotel was a neutral place for us to relearn how to be together without the emotional dramas of the past. Plus, I wasn't eager to leave the lipstick painting on the bathroom mirror. It wasn't something we could take with us when we checked out.

We continued to go to work during the week days, walking together to the bustling office building on Park Avenue. It felt good to return to my studio, to my quiet, peaceful place of creation. While we were apart, Price concentrated on his Vancouver bridge design, and I dreamed up new adornments for the Pan-Asia retail market.

Then we came together again, and we knew as soon as we embraced that what we had was worth every ounce of effort we were putting into fixing our shit. We spent our nights and weekends having sex, yes, and playing plenty of power exchange games, but we also spent time getting to know each other as people, rather than hooker and john, or Master and slave.

We hammered out the rough spots in our relationship and hashed over our insecurities and flaws. Price learned to be patient when I took calls and meetings with male clients, and accepted that I would meet with Andrew whenever and wherever I pleased during my free time. As for me, I learned not to lose faith when his insecurities caused tension between us. I beat the fears back and confronted him, we talked, we moved on.

As for the cameras at my studio and the apartment, they stayed in place, because he had a serious spying fetish, and I had nothing to hide. Not anymore.

After two weeks of this reconnecting bliss, Vinod returned from India bearing spices for Price, and dozens of half-melted candy bars. He brought me a blue and brown pashmina shawl with colors strikingly similar to mine and Price's eyes.

"I knew your separation wouldn't last," he scoffed as I draped the shawl around my shoulders. "You belong together, you two."

Jino's frown communicated silent agreement. He muttered a string of foreign syllables to Vinod, who laughed and nodded.

"What did he say?" I asked Vinod.

"He said we were idiots," replied Price.

"Idiots to believe you could be apart." Vinod held up a hand in explanation. "The word in Hindi is not precisely as rude as—"

"Whatever," I said, glaring at Jino.

Vinod laughed again at Jino's impassive expression. "Please, don't take offense at his plain way of speaking. I keep him on for his bodyguarding talents, not his charm."

"Bodyguarding talents. Right," Price said, rolling his eyes. One of the things we had talked about between frenzied bouts of sex was the way love came in all forms, whether societally accepted or not. Even if Vinod and Jino couldn't openly share their love within the strictures of Indian society, it was still there, and it had every right to exist.

In addition to saffron and chocolate, early February brought a letter from Simon's lawyers. Price handed it to me one evening and hovered over my shoulder as I opened it. I scanned the cordial greeting and paragraphs full of legal words about Simon's last will and testament. They mentioned a codicil, and the legal parameters of artistic value, and taxes and titles, and unsold works, specifically *Heart-Lust*. Even though I had no legal or marital ties to Simon, I started to panic.

"Are they asking me for money?"

"No," said Price. "They're giving you a painting, although there'll be tax repercussions. All Simon's unsold and unfinished works were left to a family trust except for one, which he bequeathed to you."

I stared at the letter. "*Heart-Lust*? I thought that belonged to the Louvre."

"They never bought it, they only displayed it. It still legally belongs to Simon. Well, now it belongs to you." Price took the papers from my hands and looked at them more closely. "It's worth a lot of money, starshine."

When Price said something was worth a lot of money in a hushed and shocked voice, that meant it was really worth a lot of fucking money.

"I guess you'll want me to sell it," I said.

He shrugged. "We can deal with the taxes."

"No, because it's Simon's, and you hate Simon."

He folded the letter and gave it back to me. "As long as it stays in Paris, it's fine. I don't want his painting hanging in our apartment, but he did create it for you. I hate him, but I respect that he found you art worthy. *Heart-Lust* was one of the few decent things he ever did for you." He nodded at the letter. "And it was generous of him to leave it to you in his will. Once you pay the taxes, you're going to own a piece of art history that's going to continue to go up in value. His work will bring Warhol prices one day, and his early stuff will probably bring more."

I was amazed for two reasons. First, that Price wasn't angry or jealous over Simon's generosity, and second, that he was actually giving him credit for something he'd done.

"I wonder when he decided to do this," I mused, running my fingers over the law office letterhead. "I mean, why not leave it to his family with all the others?"

"Maybe, even through the drug haze, he realized it belonged to you. That it would have the most meaning to you."

I gave Price a look. "You're taking this very calmly."

"I've changed." He took the letter from me, put it down on the table, and led me toward the bed. "I love you, Chere. I'm happy for you, and I'm not jealous about the painting anymore. I understand how you could drive anyone to make art." He flicked a glance toward the bathroom, where his lipstick-art poem remained undisturbed, his own heart and his own lust on a silver-reflective canvas. I'd taken a dozen photos of it, so I could keep the memory forever. I was happy about inheriting Simon's painting, but much happier about the love I found in Price's arms.

"Are you going to do it to me?" I asked, as he hooked a finger in my collar.

"The idea crossed my mind." He exerted not-so-gentle pressure to force me down between his legs. "But first, you're going to do it to me."

I opened my mouth and welcomed his rough, demanding thrusts, even when he made me gag a little. It wouldn't be Price if he wasn't gagging me. It wouldn't be his power and girth, and the sense of panic that came with serving him. He kept his fingertip hooked in my collar so I couldn't pull away or alter the rhythm he set. That was the wonderful thing about Price. He always let me know exactly what he wanted.

When he finally released me, I came up drooling and gasping for air. He flipped me over and shoved my face down into the sheets, and held me by the neck as he thrust into me from behind. He didn't say a word, didn't negotiate or suggest, he merely bent me to his will—and it felt like heaven. Even without the dungeon and all his torture instruments, he had no problem making me feel utterly surrendered and ecstatically hot.

"Please. Oh God," I groaned into the sheets. "Oh, please."

"You going to come already, little slave girl?" he asked. "Don't dare. Not yet."

When I tried to reach down and stroke my clit, he captured my hands and forced them over my head.

"Yes, I've been letting you get away with that the last couple weeks, but I think it's time we got back on track. Who gets to touch you and make you feel good?"

I arched up, pressing my back to his chest. "You, Sir. Only you."

"That's right. Who owns your pussy?" he asked, squeezing my mons in rough fingers.

"You, Sir."

"Who owns your mouth and your asshole, to use whenever he fucking wants?"

Oh, shit, I was going to come from this litany alone. "You, Sir," I wailed. "Please, it feels so good. I just forgot for a moment."

"Then I'll have to remind you, after we're finished, what happens to naughty girls who try to stroke their clits without permission."

"Yes, Sir," I said, with equal parts misery and joy. I knew what happened to naughty girls who stroked their clits without permission, at least back in the dungeon. Ten hard punishment strokes, and a night in the chastity belt with dildos in that naughty girl's pussy and ass. I wasn't going to enjoy those strokes—or the chastity—but I was thrilled that he was getting back to our old rules. When I'd said I didn't want that part of him to change, I'd meant it. I wanted him to control me sexually, to the deepest extent he wished.

I leaned down and kissed the hand planted next to me on the bed. His other hand was still clasped over my mons. His fingers teased my engorged clit, making my hips jump at the delicious trails of sensation.

"Don't come yet," he said again, and I wouldn't. I didn't dare, or I'd get more than ten strokes with whatever implement he pulled out of his travel bag. Quite a few of them had migrated over to the Gramercy during our stay, and they were mostly the quiet ones. Nylon switches, canes, thin whips, and Lucite tilt wands. Ouch.

"Who do you belong to?" Price asked as his strokes deepened. "Tell me again who owns this body."

"You do, Sir."

"Arch your hips up. I'm going to come, and then you can come too, if you can manage it before I'm through."

Oh, shit, oh, shit. He was holding my hands on the bed again so I couldn't stroke myself. I jerked back against him as he pounded me. His balls banged against my swollen clit, and along with his rough possession, it was enough to send me over the edge into a mercurial orgasm. I felt his thick organ pulsing inside me as he came at the same time. He made a growling sound of satisfaction and tightened his hands on my wrists. Who needed manacles? I felt as tightly bound as any prisoner, except, unlike a prisoner, I liked being captured.

Even if I was about to be punished.

"Don't move," he said as he pulled away from me. "Keep that ass in the air, bad girl."

"Yes, Sir."

I stuck my ass up high. Hell, I deserved it. I knew the rules, and now that I knew he was starting to enforce them more strictly, it would make everything easier. My pussy was his. My pleasure was his. Any punishment I deserved was his to dole out.

He came back with the short, whippy rattan cane, and while I made a sound of dread into the bedsheets, that was the extent of my protest.

"Are you ready?" he asked, tapping the cane against my ass.

"Yes, Sir."

"Count them for me. I don't want to hear anything but counting, and *Yes, Sir.*"

"Yes, Sir."

The first stroke whipped across my ass cheeks. I tensed and drew my legs together. *Ow, ow, ow.* "One, Sir."

The second one fell just above the first, and the third below it. I trembled with the effort to be still and quiet. The fourth one brought a wail.

"*Owwww.* Four, Sir."

"Get that ass up. This is what happens to girls who try to touch themselves without permission, isn't it?"

"Yes, Sir. *Ahh!* Five, Sir."

"We've taken a little time away from real life—"

"Six, Sir!"

"But now it's time to get back to some rules and discipline."

"*Oww.* Yes, Sir. Seven, Sir."

My ass was on fire with seven throbbing cane tracks, and the next was on the way. "Eight, Sir," I choked out when it fell.

"Nine, Sir" was so painful that I lost my composure and collapsed on the bed. He gave me one warning tap, and I hustled to my knees and stuck my ass out, because anything that counted as resistance earned five extra strokes. I gripped the sheets and cried out at the last stroke, which was always the hardest.

"Ten, Sir."

"Look at me."

I turned around to stare up at my disciplinarian, my owner, my Master. My cheeks burned hot beneath my tears.

"Are you going to be a good girl now?" he asked.

"Yes, Sir."

Oh yes, Sir. I want this. I want you and your authority and your rough love forever.

Later, after dinner, he assembled the chastity belt, then traced the ten cane welts as he held me over his lap. "I think we'll be ready to go back

178

home soon," he said. "What do you think? Do you feel ready to try again?"

"Yes, Sir. I'm definitely ready."

"You won't miss the Gramercy? All this luxury?"

I gave a little feline stretch of pleasure as he ran a hand up my back. "As long as you're there, I'll be happy."

He laughed. "I don't know why I make you happy. I'm so cruel to you." He slapped my poor, wet clit and slid the first of the chastity dildos into my pussy. It was thick and textured, to tease me all night, and my body couldn't help squeezing on the ribbed surface. It felt good. Horribly good, because I wasn't allowed to come. He forced me to be still as he inserted the anal dildo next. As much as I was used to this treatment, I moaned at the invasive ache. It was also thick, and since it attached to the belt, there was no narrower neck for my sphincter to contract around. It kept me open and worked up all night.

Shit, he'd also used the itching lube. Back to the old life. Back to the old rules. No more Mr. Nice Guy.

But that was okay. As he fitted the curved metal plate over my aching clit and locked me up for the night, I felt like everything was just as it was supposed to be. He was in control, but he loved me, and he would keep me safe.

He put me on my knees to suck him off one last time before bed. He always got hard when he put me into chastity. I got hard too, but oh well. Since I wasn't allowed to come, or even beg to come the way I wanted, I put all my energy into serving him. I got my reward later, when he held me and kissed my forehead as I drifted off to sleep.

"I'm going to dream about you," he whispered. "My beautiful, good girl."

* * * * *

Chere and I checked out of the Gramercy Park Hotel on Valentine's Day. It seemed the most appropriate day to do it, since both of us were hopeless romantics. We'd done a lot of relationship work at the Gramercy, and had the peace of mind to show for it. I was glad now that she'd run away from me, since it forced us to face our issues head on.

Even so, I was nervous about our first trip back to the dungeon. I'd fixed the gouges in the wall where I'd thrown the cage, but the cage itself still lay on its side where it had fallen. I didn't want to gloss over the things that had happened between us. I didn't want to tidy away the evidence, at least not yet.

It wasn't long after we returned home that Chere asked to visit the scene of our unraveling. I took her hand and led her inside the gray-walled room so we could face the demons together. I didn't require nudity or speech restriction. For this conversation, we needed to be equals, not Master and slave.

"It looks the same." She sounded surprised as she wandered toward the center of the space. "You haven't changed anything."

"No. I was waiting for you." I joined her as we both turned toward the far wall. "In my opinion, there's only one thing that really needs to go."

"The sawhorse?" she asked hopefully, but she knew what I meant.

We crossed to the cage. She traced the metal bars with a mournful expression.

"It's a shame," I said. "You looked so beautiful when you were in there."

"We don't have to..." she said tentatively. "I mean, if you want to keep it."

I shook my head. "Maybe we can have one again later. When a little time has passed, and we trust ourselves more."

"You're right. This one has too much bad juju attached to it."

"Not bad juju." I leaned over the cage and pulled out the first of the long, cylindrical end pins. "I was the one who did the bad thing. The cage was just doing its job." I pulled out a second end pin, holding the structure so it wouldn't collapse.

"That's it?" she said as the panels rattled loose. "That's all you have to do to put this cage together and take it apart? Just pull out those rods?"

"It's a basic design. It held up, yeah?" I gave her a lopsided grin. "I'm a good engineer." Just to mess with her, I turned one of the metal rods over in my hands. "Maybe we can find a use for this."

She took it from me. "Uh, no. Remember? Bad juju."

"How can you say it's bad?" I asked, taking the rod back and carrying it with the others out toward the living room. "We learned a lot because of this cage. It definitely brought us to a better place."

"After a bunch of violence and drama," she called after me.

When I returned, she helped me pick up each panel and carry it out to the living room, where we stacked them against the wall.

"Think you can use these at your studio?" I asked. "Melt them down into other things? It's good metal. Stainless steel and brass."

She traced the gleaming bars as I stared at her fingers, their only adornment the delicate garnet ring. I thought about commitment and ownership, the healthy kind, not the captive-in-a-tower kind that really only existed in fairy tales. "Maybe you can make a ring with it," I said, taking her hand. "An engagement ring."

"I prefer that to making manacles. But stainless steel for an engagement ring?"

I let go of her hand and grabbed her ass. "I guess gold and diamonds are more traditional. I'll buy the materials, you make the ring. How about that?"

"Yes, Sir," she said, looking adorably pleased.

Now that that was out of the way, I dragged her back into the dungeon. It looked better. It looked ready for us to begin again. "So," I said, rubbing my hands together. "You've missed the sawhorse, I gather."

"No, I haven't missed it at al—"

"And where are those manacles you mentioned?"

"We just got back," she pleaded.

"Quiet, slave. I suppose it's time to revert to speech restriction again."

Chere was rescued by the sound of the doorbell. She turned and ran out of the dungeon. "I'll get it," she yelled over her shoulder.

Ha. She had a date with the sawhorse and manacles whether she liked it or not, but I hadn't really intended to play with her yet. I was expecting a delivery from the Gramercy Park Hotel. By the time I got out to the living room, four burly delivery guys with white gloves were easing a wrapped and padded rectangle through the door.

"Do you know what it is?" I asked Chere.

She looked puzzled as I directed the men to leave the package propped against the far wall. I'd have to have someone come in to mount it. All families needed a portrait over the fireplace. This would be ours, because it would always force us to see our reflections. We'd never let things go haywire again.

"Go ahead," I said. "Open the wrapping. Just a corner. You'll figure it out."

She peeled back an edge of padding and brown craft paper. She drew in a breath as she saw her own eyes staring back at her.

"The mirror from the Gramercy. Oh, wow. And you let me cry and take a billion more photos of it this morning."

"You know I love when you cry."

She turned to me and made a face that transformed into a smile. "I'm so glad you kept it. I'm amazed they let you keep it!"

"I have some friends on staff." I drew her back and kissed her hard on her beautiful lips. "Happy Valentine's Day."

"All I got you were some cuff links," she protested.

"And that ring you're going to make me, out of diamonds and gold, so I can give it back to you."

She giggled as I kissed her again. "I'm not sure you know how this whole gift giving thing works."

"Oh, I know how it works." *Mine also, little painted poem of God.* The universe had brought me a gift, and she was in my arms, and she was worth any fucking price.

As for the mirror, sure, it was expensive to take one from the Gramercy, and have a new one installed in its place, but Chere loved my poetry, and this one might end up being the most important poem of all.

That is, after her.

CHAPTER EIGHTEEN: THREE YEARS LATER

Price and I were in Vancouver, at a quiet park overlooking an inlet. In the distance, a spare, glittering bridge spanned the water and touched down lightly on the opposite shore. As the city constructed it, people used words like *groundbreaking* and *game-changing* to describe the minimalist design. A few people had called it plain, or ugly, but they were idiots.

My husband didn't do plain or ugly. He made works of art.

"Wow," I said, watching the sun glint off the slender posts and wires. "Wow. I have no words. It's breathtaking, baby. How did you do that? I mean, the balance. The symmetry. The design."

"I had a lot of inspiration." He corralled me into a hug and a rough, quick kiss. "I only wish they would have let me name the damn thing."

"The Chere Rouzier-Eriksen Bridge would have been a real tongue twister."

"So's the name of that politician they named it after." He shrugged. "Whatever. It'll always be the Chere Bridge to me."

"I'm honored. Seriously, I think it's the most beautiful thing you've made so far."

"No, not quite. It doesn't compare to this work of art." He scooped up our daughter as she toddled past, and pressed his nose to hers. "Does it, sunshine? You're the most beautiful thing in the universe. Well, the most beautiful two year old, anyway." He threw a sideways wink in my direction.

"Nice save," I said. "And I hate to point it out, but you didn't actually make her."

He put a hand over Aliya's kinky ponytail curls. "Hush. She'll hear you."

I grinned at the striking contrast of his daughter's dark coloring against his pale Nordic skin. "She's going to figure it out one day, blondie. But for now I'll play along, because yes, she's absolutely beautiful."

"Mama," she cooed, reaching out for me with grassy, grubby fingers. But as soon as she was in my arms, she reached again for Price. "Daddy. Want Daddy."

He took her, grubby fingers and all, and tossed her up in the air, to avid screeches of approval. Aliya had been adopted into our family almost a year ago. I'd been scared about passing on my parents' mental health genes, and Price wasn't jazzed about giving up my body for the length of a pregnancy, so we'd looked into adopting a child. Since both of us had gotten second chances, we decided we wanted to give an at-risk child a second chance too.

Our adopted daughter had had a rough start in life, like me, but she was also a fighter, like me. Add in Price's protectiveness, and his mission to do better than his parents, and our little sunshine was definitely going to take over the world, along with the sibling we planned to adopt in a year or two. Our daughter also had Andrew and Craig for fairy godfathers. Andrew had painted her first portrait last month, and given it to us as an anniversary present. He'd captured all the warmth and light in her young face. We had so much love between us, and Aliya seemed to multiply it every day.

As for her effect on our dynamic, well, the dungeon was soundproof. I was so glad Price had been thinking ahead.

"Let mama wash your hands," I said, digging in the diaper bag for wipes.

"No wash."

"They're dirty. Let mama wash Aya's hands."

"No wash A-ya's hands," she repeated, this time with an emphatic shake of her head. She was in that stage where everything was no, even when she meant yes. Price said she took after me in her stubbornness, but I thought she took after him. Actually, it was probably just a two-year-old thing.

"Let her dig a while longer," he said, letting her down. "Maybe we have a future geologist on our hands."

We sat on a nearby bench and let her scratch out a series of toddler-sized holes. When she got tired of that, she started pulling up grass, arranging it in random piles.

"She's making excellent use of negative design space," Price murmured.

I laughed and rested my head against his shoulder. "I never imagined life could feel like this," I said in the silence that followed. "I never thought I could have all this. I never thought there was a way."

"There's always a way." He squeezed my hand. "Life works like this, Chere: you get what you deserve. We deserved each other."

"No, we found each other, by chance and by luck," I said. "And then we had to fight for what we had."

"Which is why we deserve what we have now. It took a lot of hard work, and a lot of risk." He gestured toward the distance. "Like that bridge over there. But it's worth it, isn't it?"

"Yes, Sir," I said softly. "It is."

"I almost sent you away that day," he said, turning back to me. "The first day, at the W Hotel. I wanted a blonde."

"I was blonde back then."

He touched my dark brown hair. "I wanted a natural blonde. I'm glad I finally figured out that I was looking for the wrong thing."

He was kind enough not to point it out, but I'd been looking for the wrong thing too, for ten miserable years. Wow. We'd really worked hard to change, to get better, to give the love we shared today a fighting chance.

Aliya bounded over and deposited a handful of grass shards on Price's knee.

"Are these diamonds?" he asked, regarding them with gravity. "Did you bring Daddy diamonds?"

She nodded with a pleased, gap-toothed grin. "Di-mons."

She was a jeweler's daughter. She knew what diamonds were. She loved how they sparkled, like the solitaire in my engagement ring. She

185

loved that ring more than the garnet ring I still wore, but she didn't know the story behind it. I thought I'd always love the garnet ring a little more.

She ran away and came back with another handful of grass, and placed it reverently in my lap.

"Di-mons, mama."

"I see."

"Beautiful diamond," said Price against my ear. "Beautiful heart."

I teared up whenever he quoted that poem. I ducked my head to hide it, but he laughed and made me look at him anyway. There was no hiding from him, which I supposed was good. Aliya spun away and ran off again, singing about diamonds and pulling up more grass.

There was always a way, if you wanted it badly enough. We'd fought for what we wanted, and now it was ours.

A FINAL NOTE

I have so many people to thank for their help with the Rough Love trilogy. First of all, I have to thank the readers who badgered me to write it, even when I doubted. (Sometimes rough love works.)

Thanks to Ay and Roughinamorato for providing some nitty gritty details about the rougher stuff, as well as the numerous Fetlife friends who've inspired me with their edgier kinks through the years. Thanks to Riane Holt for saving *Taunt Me* when I wanted to ball it up and set it on fire, and to my other trusty editors and beta readers, Lina of LinaEdits.com, Audrey, Doris, Tiffany, Janine, Tasha, Tracy, and Linda.

Thanks to Kate at Bad Star Media for the trio of sexy covers, and to Nina, Irene, and the Literary Gossip ladies for launch help. Mega thanks to all the Club Annabel denizens for being my goddesses of encouragement. I won't name names, because if I leave anyone out by accident I'll be crushed, but you know who you are.

Thanks finally to Price and Chere, who came into my mind fully formed, as imperfect as they were, and kept me writing even when it seemed too dark to go on. I hope they're pleased with their happily ever after, and I hope you are too. If you would be so kind as to leave online reviews, and help spread the word about the Rough Love series in your naughty reading groups, I'd be ever so grateful.

You can learn more about my other series by signing up for my newsletter at annabeljoseph.com, or following me on Facebook or Twitter. You can also apply to join Club Annabel on Facebook if you're looking for an AJ discussion and social group. I'm so grateful for your support.

COMING SOON:
THE PROBLEM PRINCESS,
BOOK ONE IN THE ROYAL DISCIPLINE SERIES

There's a problem in the kingdom of Hastings: the princess is too headstrong and ill-mannered to carry on the royal line. In desperation, the king delivers his daughter to the darkly imposing Duke of Thornton, who promises to correct her behavior through a course of stringent and lowering physical chastisement.

Despite the duke's harsh disciplinary measures, Princess Violet resists change, and Thornton is drawn into an escalating battle of wills with his spirited charge. How far will he go to humble the haughty royal, and put an end to her spoiled behavior? This fairy tale fantasy is a raunchy tumble into spanking depravity, with a royally satisfying ending.

YOU MAY ALSO ENJOY THESE OTHER BDSM SERIES BY ANNABEL JOSEPH

THE FORTUNE SERIES

Deep in the Woods... Sophie finally finds the courage to reenter the BDSM scene after extricating herself from an abusive relationship. At a local munch, she meets Dave, a funny, laid-back erotic photographer. They embark on a thrilling D/s relationship and Sophie finds healing and fulfillment in Dave's arms.

But Sophie is still haunted by nightmares of her past. On a dark night in the woods with Dave and his friend Ryan, frightening memories overtake her. She knows that in order to move on, she must uncover the tragedy that haunts her subconscious.

Sophie's quest for answers brings her face-to-face with her previous tormentor. She finds herself once more in the deep woods, not only fighting for answers, but also for her life.

Fortune... Kat doesn't know how to end her six-night-a-week party habit, not to mention her unhealthy addiction to meaningless sex. Then an accident lands her in the hospital. She wakes to a menagerie of origami figures, and a gorgeous neurosurgeon beside her bed. The complexity of the paper creations is nothing compared to the complexity of dark-eyed, authoritative Ryan, who seems determined to give her life some direction. Trouble is, Kat's just as determined to resist his efforts to tame her wild side.

With persistence, Ryan draws Kat into his world of dominance and submission, where quiet commands and lengths of rope awaken needs and desires she never knew she possessed. But Ryan's erotic shibari sessions frighten Kat as much as they excite her, for each simple knot requires infinite trust and inspires complicated emotions.

When a family crisis threatens to snap the fragile ties that bind them, will fortune smile on this unlikely couple, or will fate tear them apart?

Reader Advisory: For those who subscribe to a "more the merrier" philosophy, this story contains a scintillating m/f/f/m scene.

THE BDSM BALLET SERIES

Waking Kiss... A stranger in the wings, a traitorous pair of toe shoes, and a traumatic turn dancing with The Great Rubio... For ballerina Ashleigh Keaton, it's been one hell of a night.

But it's not over yet. When Rubio drags her to a private party at his friend's house in the ritzy part of London, she meets Liam Wilder, a lifestyle dominant and frighteningly seductive man. Liam pursues Ashleigh, attracted by her strength and talent, but she has secrets—an abusive past and a crippling fear of intimacy that prevents her from connecting to anyone, especially a playboy reputed to be legendary in bed.

Eventually he wins her trust and sets out to heal the troubled dancer, awakening her to a world of sensual abandon in a series of BDSM "sessions" at his home. But how pure are his motives? Is he helping her or endangering her fragile soul? Liam hides his own destructive secrets, and so does Fernando Rubio, their temperamental friend. Over time the three become embroiled in a tangle of artifice, fears, and lies that threaten to undo everything they've worked for.

Will Ashleigh and Liam find the strength to defeat their demons? Or are they cursed to sleepwalk through life forever, afraid to experience the passion and intimacy of love?

Fever Dream... Petra Hewitt's the top ballerina in the world, and The Great Rubio her obvious counterpart, so why does she want to strangle him whenever he's around? He's haughty, abrupt, demanding— and alarmingly sexy. Petra knows Rubio is dangerous to her heart, to her peace of mind, and worst of all, to her career, but his rough flirtation compels her. When she gets a chance to play with him at a BDSM party, their professional partnership takes a feverish left turn.

After that, any attempts to keep him at arm's length falter in the face of his obstinate sexuality. Rubio's methods are ruthlessly erotic as he introduces her to the pleasures of sadism, bondage, pain, and submission. The more Petra tries to resist him, the more she craves his strength and control.

But as they play their sensual games of dominance and submission, career pressures mount, and an overzealous fan brings dangerous tension to their relationship. Soon, the dream gives way to the stark reality of her vulnerability. Maybe, just maybe, some risks are too terrifying to take.

Like it Rough?
You may also enjoy these edgy BDSM romances by Annabel Joseph

The Cirque Masters series

Enter a world where performers' jaw-dropping strength, talent, and creativity is matched only by the decadence of their kinky desires. Cirque du Monde is famous for mounting glittering circus productions, but after the Big Top goes dark, you can find its denizens at *Le Citadel*, a fetish club owned by Cirque CEO Michel Lemaitre—where anything goes. This secret world is ruled by dominance and submission, risk and emotion, and a fearless dedication to carnal pleasure in all its forms. Love in the circus can be as perilous as aerial silks or trapeze, and secrets run deep in this intimate society. Run away to the circus, and soar with the Cirque Masters—a delight for the senses, and for the heart.

The Cirque Masters series is:
#1 *Cirque de Minuit* (Theo's story)
#2 *Bound in Blue* (Jason's story)
#3 *Master's Flame* (Lemaitre's story)

The Club Mephisto series

Club Mephisto... Molly is a 24/7 slave dedicated to serving her Master. When business calls him away on a weeklong trip, he arranges to leave her in the care of Mephisto, the owner of a thriving local BDSM club. Molly is both excited and scared to be given over to Master Mephisto. His power and mysterious intensity have long compelled her from afar.

She finds herself immersed in a world of strict commands, pervasive sex, and creative torments. Over the course of a week, Mephisto strips away privileges Molly took for granted, and forces her to understand and acknowledge the depths to which she can be made to submit. But a surprising conversation the last day threatens Molly's worldview, as does the strange closeness that develops between them. As the time of Master's return draws near, Molly finds herself deeply and inexorably changed.

Note: this BDSM fantasy novella depicts "total power exchange" relationships that some readers may find objectionable. This work contains acts of sadism, objectification, orgasm denial and speech restriction, caging, anal play and double penetration, BDSM punishment and discipline, M/f, M/m/f, M/m, orgy and group sexual encounters, voyeurism, and limited circumstances of dubious consent.

Molly's Lips: Club Mephisto Retold... If you've read *Club Mephisto*, you know the story from Molly's perspective. Now, prepare to relive the experience from Mephisto's point of view in this gripping novella.

When Mephisto's friend Clayton is called out of town on business, he agrees to look after his slave for the week. But Molly isn't your average slave. She and Clayton share a serious, full time dynamic. Mephisto feels a weight of responsibility he isn't used to, and worse, an intense attraction to Molly, the partner of his friend.

Mephisto is determined to sublimate his inappropriate desires and provide a challenging and instructive week for the devoted slave. He subjects Molly to orgasm denial, speech restriction, scenes of erotic torment, even an orgy where she is made to service his friends. Along the way, he experiences unfamiliar jealousy, and deep cravings to possess her himself.

Throughout the week, he is also haunted by persistent questions. Is she happy being a 24/7 slave? Or is there another Molly trapped beneath her submissive, surrendered gaze?

Burn For You... When Molly loses her longtime Master, she feels lost, angry. Confused. She's unsure of her future, even her calling to the BDSM lifestyle. She knows her Master always intended her to go to his friend Mephisto next, but their emotionally—and sexually—fraught history is still a confusion of desire and fear in her mind.

Mephisto wants to help Molly, but he doesn't want to force her into service she's not sure she wants. He owes it to Clayton to help her find happiness, but how? Molly and Mephisto advance and retreat from one another as they try to untangle their complex feelings. More and more it seems their tense standoff will only end one way...

Note: this 63K-word erotic romance novel contains consensual BDSM play, Master/slavery, sado-masochism, anal play, objectification, caging, and other consensual activities which some might find offensive.

The Mephisto series is:
#1 *Club Mephisto* (Molly's POV)
#2 *Molly's Lips* (Mephisto's POV)
#3 *Burn For You* (the romantic conclusion)

THE COMFORT SERIES

Have you ever wondered what goes on in the bedrooms of Hollywood's biggest heartthrobs? In the case of Jeremy Gray, the reality is far more depraved than anyone realizes. Brutal desires, shocking secrets, and a D/s relationship (with a hired submissive "girlfriend") that's based on a contract rather than love. It's just the beginning of a four-book saga following Jeremy and his Hollywood friends as they seek comfort in fake, manufactured relationships. Born of necessity—and public relations— these attachments come to feel more and more real. What does it take to live day-to-day with an A-list celebrity? Patience, fortitude, and a whole lot of heart. Oh, and a *very* good pain tolerance for kinky mayhem.

Comfort series is:
#1 *Comfort Object* (Jeremy's story)
#2 *Caressa's Knees* (Kyle's story)
#3 *Odalisque* (Kai's story)
#4 *Command Performance* (Mason's story)

About the Author

Annabel Joseph is a multi-published, New York Times Bestselling BDSM romance author. She writes mainly contemporary romance, although she has been known to dabble in the medieval and Regency eras. She is known for writing emotionally intense BDSM storylines, and strives to create characters that seem real—even flawed—so readers are better able to relate to them. Annabel also writes non-BDSM romance under the pen name Molly Joseph.

You can follow Annabel on Twitter (@annabeljoseph) or Facebook (facebook.com/annabeljosephnovels), or sign up to receive her monthly newsletter at annabeljoseph.com. She also loves to hear from her readers at annabeljosephnovels@gmail.com.